HARD JUSTICE

THE LEGEND OF JASPER LEE

A NOVEL
BY
Mike McNeff

Whidbey
Writers
Group Press

Copyright 2014, 2016 Mike McNeff

This work is licensed under a Creative Commons Attribution-Noncommercial-No Derivative Works 3.0 Unported License.

Attribution — You must attribute the work in the manner specified by the author or licensor (but not in any way that suggests that they endorse you or your use of the work).

Noncommercial — You may not use this work for commercial purposes.

No Derivative Works — You may not alter, transform, or build upon this work.

Inquiries about additional permissions should be directed to: wwgpress@gmail.com

Cover Design by Greg Simanson
Edited by Hanna Barnes

This is a work of fiction. Names, characters, places, brands, media, and incidents are either the product of the author's imagination or are used fictitiously. Any resemblance to similarly named places or to persons living or deceased is unintentional.

Print ISBN 978-1-944215-02-6

EPUB ISBN 978-1-944215-03-3

Second Edition

DISCOUNTS OR CUSTOMIZED EDITIONS MAY BE AVAILABLE FOR EDUCATIONAL AND OTHER GROUPS BASED ON BULK PURCHASE.

For further information please contact wwgpress@gmail.com

Library of Congress Control Number: 2014930793

Whidbey Writers Group Press is a d/b/a of Whidbey Writers Group, LLC

For Mom, Kay McNeff,

who was loved by everyone she ever met.

Acknowledgments

I have stories and characters in my head banging to get out, so I have to write. But I doubt I would have grown as a writer without my team and friends. I hope to continue to grow with their support.

First and foremost is my content editor, Hanna Barnes. Our author/editor relationship had somewhat of a bumpy start as we learned about each other. From that uncertain beginning we've evolved into a richly rewarding collaboration.

My copy editors, Cathy Shaw and Michaelene McElroy keep the i's dotted and the t's crossed along with the rest of the pesky little details that often escape me.

A special thanks to novelist Ruby Standing Deer for her insights into Native American culture and lore.

To my writing friends who offer a place to bounce ideas off of and compare notes, resources and other crazy things writers worry about, my deepest gratitude. They are everybody at Whidbey Writers Group and Mare, Derrick, Niki, Brian, Mare and Rowena.

To one of the best, Gordon Labuhn, keep fighting Gordon and get well.

To the most special of all, my wife Linda. Thank you for everything you are and do. I'm the luckiest guy in the world.

Hard Crimes

EZRA LEE AND HIS TWO YOUNGER SONS rode their horses lazily in the cool of the early morning. The fragrance of newly sprouted prairie grass announced spring. Ezra, a stern, but good man, rode tall in his saddle.

Young Caleb had an easy smile on his face as he watched two eagles make graceful circles. He thought how wonderful it would be to fly like such a graceful bird. He caught the grin on Jonas' face, who shook his head at Caleb's daydreaming. The men had just reached the north edge of the town of Arlington when a woman's scream shattered the quiet of the just awakening community. They urged their horses forward, cutting between two buildings toward Dolan's Livery Stables.

A score of outlaws had pretty Claire Dolan surrounded. A pail of spilled milk muddied the ground. Two men held Claire by her arms, her eyes wide with terror. Ezra raised his Sharps .50 caliber rifle to his shoulder and charged the outlaws. His sons rode on either side, close and slightly behind, pistols in hand.

"Unhand that young girl!" Ezra yelled.

A dozen pistols and again as many rifles pointed at the three men challenging the criminals. Smoke, fire and lead roared. An onslaught of bullets blasted Jonas' head into a cloud of crimson mist and Caleb, the youngest and smallest of the Lee boys, drew ragged breaths through a hole in his rib cage.

Bullets hit Ezra hard laying him low on his mare, but the horse bucked at the gunfire. Ezra thumped hard onto the ground.

Caleb struggled to his feet and staggered to his father. "Pa!" he cried and collapsed on his dad.

Ezra croaked out a hoarse whisper, "Run, Caleb. Get help."

Eldon Samson trotted his horse up to the two wounded men. "Well, an old man and a whippersnapper. How come you're so stupid old man? Did you really think you could take on us gunfighters?"

"Gunfighters?" Ezra laughed through his pain. "You're nothing but pond scum."

"And you're nothing but dead." Samson pointed his pistol at Ezra's head.

Caleb lurched up toward Samson, the blade of a Bowie knife flashing in the sunlight. He thought of his big brother, who gave him his knife, and what Jasper would do. Caleb plunged the knife into Samson's thigh. Samson yelled and shot Caleb in the face, point blank, causing the back of his head to explode blood, bone and brain.

"Goddamn, little bastard!" Samson yelled. He sucked in a lung full of air and yanked the knife out of his leg. He held it up and looked at it for a second and then tossed it next to Caleb's body. Pointing his pistol at Ezra he said, "Here's for that little son of a bitch." He shot Ezra twice in the chest and then carefully aimed and shot him in the head.

"Get the girl on a horse!" Bart Moore yelled. "We need to get outta here."

Claire screamed in her struggle against the man trying to lift her onto a horse. She kicked his shin hard.

"Bitch." He struck her in the face with a closed fist and she went limp.

"Stop!" A shout came from the back of Finley's Dry Goods.

Bullets started flying and Charlie Finley ducked back into his store.

"Let's go!" Moore ordered and the men galloped off.

Chapter One

JASPER LEE CAME FROM BEHIND HIS LOG HOME carrying an armload of newly split wood and squinted into the warm, brilliant early May afternoon. Sheriff Carl Williams sat on his horse at the gate. His horse dug at the ground with his hooves. Nervous horse. Nervous rider.

"Howdy, Carl. What brings you all the way out here?"

The sheriff dismounted, looped his reins over the hitching rail and came through the gate. He removed his hat. "I have news, Jasper...bad news."

Jasper stooped and stacked the logs at the end of the woodpile. "Well, you better come in and tell it."

"No, Jasper." the sheriff lowered his voice, "I think this news best not be told in front of your family." His hands twisted and bent the wide brim of his Stetson. "Jasper, your pa and brothers were shot and killed this mornin'."

Jasper slowly rose. "What happened?"

"They tried to save young Claire Dolan from being taken by outlaws, but the outlaws still took her."

Jasper stood mute until the manners his stepmother taught him took hold and forced out the words that stuck in his throat. "Thank you, Carl. I know things like this are hard to do. Thank you for comin'."

"We're forming a posse. We'd welcome you."

Jasper set his right foot on the porch. His left knee felt weak as water and he clasped the railing and forced himself to stand firm. "I believe I have some buryin' to do. After that, I'll be my own posse."

"Now, Jasper, you can't go after these men alone. You've settled down. You have a family."

"Nothin' against you, Carl, but I don't trust the justice you represent."

"You're not a lawman, my friend, and it's been quite a while since you've unlimbered those Colts."

"I believe in the natural law and justice for the likes of the vermin who killed my kin."

"Jasper, the war is over. Times are changin' and the rule of law is takin' hold. The old ways are fadin'."

He wanted to scream, but Pa didn't raise him to do such things. "Not for me, Carl...not for me." Jasper turned and walked back into his home.

The Lee ranches lay side by side in the lower foothills. After a night of silent grieving and a day of digging, Jasper and his family stood on the hill overlooking the lush valley. The late afternoon sun cast a golden hue across the blue-green grass that spread out before them. Jasper thought how this scene normally made him happy and bright, but today, he only felt a harsh, hollow sadness. The hill had three fresh graves Jasper and his two sons, Sean and Brenden, had dug to bury Pa, Jonas and Caleb. Three fresh white crosses marked the graves. May 15, 1873, the date of death on each cross burned into Jasper's mind. Two older graves on either side of Pa's held Ezra's long gone wives; Mae, Jasper's mother and Liza, mother to Jonas and Caleb.

No one from town came to pay respects. The men were out with the posse and the women were too afraid to travel. Fear even kept Preacher Sunlund from doing his duties.

Jasper stood grim faced feeling older than his thirty-nine years. His wife, Gale, stood next to him, red eyed, her arm in his. Their daughters, Megan and Abbey, clung to them crying softly. Sean and Brenden stood across from the rest of the family. Brenden studying his father's face; Sean looking off in the distance.

Jasper let out a long sigh. "I believe it's time to say some words over the graves of our kin." He looked down and shuffled his feet. He knew it was his place to speak but he wasn't comfortable doing so.

"Let me, Pa," Sean said.

Jasper nodded.

Sean took a deep breath as he squared his shoulders and spread his feet a little more. "Grandpa was a good man. There's no other way to say it. He'd help anyone, always give a good word and worked hard. He loved everyone standin' here and we all loved him. I don't know anything better to say about any man.

"Jonas was not only my uncle, but also my best friend. He taught me things an uncle can that a pa can't, things a body has to know about life. I trusted him and he trusted me. I shall sorely miss him.

"Uncle Caleb taught me how to have fun and that a man's size doesn't determine how big a man he is. He was the bravest man I ever knew and he taught me to never give up. He always made me laugh and the light in our lives will be a bit dimmer without him."

Jasper looked across at his son and the ache in his heart eased a touch. He could see the beginnings of the man Sean would be. A man that Ezra would have been proud of. "Those were mighty fine words, Sean. Thank you. You make us proud."

Gale nodded with a sad smile. "I think we need to gather our things and head back home so I can fix us a supper," Gale said softly.

"Yes," Jasper turned and headed down the hill at a quick pace. "I've got to get ready to travel."

Gale caught up at the bottom of the hill. "Jasper, I'm only going to ask once. Please let the law handle this. We need you home with us."

Jasper put his arm around his wife. "You know I love you all. I don't mean to disrespect your wishes but this is my fight. These men must be brought to justice according to natural law. I got it to do."

Gale nodded her acceptance, but as Jasper helped her into the wagon a tear rolled down her cheek.

Two days of hard hurt wore heavy on Jasper but the deep blue sky above, the open range stretched out bright green before him, the pine covered foothills, and the easy motion of his horse, Coal, provided a measure of solace. Gale had cleaned and mended his buckskin shirt and his cavalry pants from the War Between the States. They fit well even after eight years. A Stetson wide brimmed Carlsbad hat protected his face and head from the sun.

Leaving his wife and four children standing on the front porch wrenched his heart. Gale's worrisome stare at the new Colts on his hips weighed on his mind but it felt good to have them on again. The one on his right hip was set for a fast draw while standing. The Colt on the left hip was set cross-draw for shooting while riding or sitting. He let his right hand slip from the saddle horn and rest on the warm wood of the also new Winchester '73 in the saddle scabbard.

The good sheriff was wrong. Jasper loved to shoot. He practiced every day with his guns. Shooting allowed him to keenly focus on a single thing. It cleared his mind and gave him respite from life's daily problems. He wore other weapons but these were not for other men to see until it became necessary. He wanted them to see his Colts.

He slowed his approach to Pody Junction, eyeing two riders coming from the north. When they hailed him and quickened the pace of their horses, he recognized two of his neighbors.

"Jasper, hard news," Micah Niles, a tall thin man with a walrus mustache said. "The posse was ambushed. The sheriff and Bob Ricks were killed. More men were wounded including Al Dolan."

"Where did this happen?"

"About four miles north of town on the Arlington Road."

"They was waitin' for us," Burt Ashton said. "Like they knew we was comin'."

"How many of the posse are still after them?"

"The posse's done," Micah said. "There's no stomach for it."

"No stomach for goin' for the girl?" Jasper's mouth hardened into a frown.

The men looked down or away.

"Ah, no matter." Jasper laid his hand back on the Winchester. "It takes a certain kind for this work."

"Well, Jasper, you was fearsome in the cattle wars," Micah said. "I imagine you're that kind."

"I'm done fightin' other men's wars. This one's my war." Jasper lifted his hat and wiped his brow. "I'd be obliged if you folks would check on my family now and again, 'til I get back."

"We'll do that," Micah replied. Burt nodded his head.

"Good day, gentlemen." Jasper's heels tapped Coal's flanks and he headed north. He skirted the town to avoid word spreading he was out and about. He threaded his way through the poplar and oak trees along Arlington Creek which ran next to the road. His eyes constantly scanned an arc ahead of him and he stopped every once in a while to check his back trail and listen. All he heard was the breeze tickling the leaves along with the gentle lullaby of the creek. A hawk cried out.

When Jasper figured he reached four miles he angled east up a rise, keeping just below the skyline. He saw no movement but a buzzard spiraling in lazy circles about a half mile away.

Easing Coal down the hill to the edge of the road, Jasper stopped. He listened, but heard nothing except flies darting around him as the day warmed. The stench of death lightly rode the breeze. He crossed the road, weaving through the boulders until he came to the area where the buzzard circled. Jasper noticed the hoof prints of maybe two dozen horses that had trampled the ground. A coyote scurried away from a brushy patch.

He dismounted and looped his reins around his saddle horn. He knew Coal wouldn't leave him and he wanted the big black stallion to be able to defend himself from other critters, if necessary. Jasper drew a Colt then moved carefully toward the brush. Pushing the brush aside revealed Claire Dolan's naked body. He walked closer but had to stop long enough to force his stomach to stay put. It wasn't what the critters had done that brought a surge of bile to his throat.

Claire's bloody face was set in contorted agony. She lay with her arms staked out and her legs splayed wide. Blood caked around her groin and the girl's breasts were skinned. The cheeks on her face were sliced away and where the light of her clear blue eyes had once sparkled, only bloodied sockets remained. Her long, golden blonde hair had fallen victim to a scalper's blade. The same blade sliced Claire's throat, the outlaws' final injustice ending Claire's suffering. Jasper had seen much violence in his life, but he shuddered at the depravity of this crime. He wrapped the body in his blanket and moved it to a clean spot by the creek where the sycamores swayed and wild flowers danced brightly, the breeze spreading their fragrance.

Jasper unpacked his camp shovel and for three hours he dug. He dug another grave. He dug it deep to protect Claire from critters scattering her around.

He stabbed the camp shovel into the fresh turned dirt so hard it sank half-way up the handle. Then, with a heavy sigh he lifted her ever so gently, as if trying not to hurt her. Stepping into the grave, he carefully laid her down.

Each shovel of dirt Jasper put over Claire tore a piece of his soul and seared into his mind. Losing his Pa and brothers was bad enough, but they died outright. Claire's agonizing death was something Jasper could not fully comprehend. It took another hour of work to satisfy Jasper the grave site was fitting for Claire, hoping when her family came to see her they would be pleased with her final resting place. He worried that they would want to move her and see the true horror of her death.

His difficult duty finished, he sat in the saddle for a full minute staring at Claire's grave until his mouth set in a grim, thin line. He took a deep breath then urged the big horse forward.

Chapter Two

JEB NORTON LOOKED UP from his plow. A buggy escorted by four horsemen rolled toward the house. He knew who they were and his stomach tightened. He wished he'd never bought land next to that man's ranch. Wrapping the reins around the plow handle, he hurried to the farmhouse, for he knew his wife's hatred for the man. He got to the door and opened it.

"Nancy!"

Nancy, a short, plump woman with shining brown hair, came out of the back room.

"What is it, Jeb?"

"Men are comin'. Stay inside."

"Who is it?"

"It's him."

Nancy's deep blue eyes flashed. "I'll not stay inside with that crooked snake in my yard!"

Jeb grabbed his wife by the shoulders. "Nancy, these men are dangerous. He's already angry because we've turned down two offers."

Nancy's lips quivered. "Jeb, you're not thinkin' of givin' up are you?"

"I don't know. I have to see what he wants. But I'll not let pride kill us."

Nancy turned and rushed into the other room.

Jeb closed the door and turned to face the oncoming men. The buggy pulled to a stop in front of him. The horsemen pushed their mounts closer, surrounding Jeb.

"Afternoon, Jeb," Cornell Norris said cheerfully. He was a tall man, powerfully built. He wore an all black suit with a long coat and an expensive black Stetson.

Jeb felt he was confronting the devil.

"Governor," Jeb nodded.

"I came to see if you've thought about my last offer."

"Governor, you know how hard Nancy and I have worked on our place. We've sacrificed much for five years and just started makin' a profit with our crops and livestock to wheres we can start a family. I ain't sayin' your offer ain't fair, but this place is our lives. Really, no offer is enough."

"I'm sorry to hear that, Jeb. See, I worry about you folks out here all by yourselves. So many things can happen; wolves, mountain lions, accidents, outlaws …"

The two men locked eyes. Jeb was working hard to suppress the seething fury inside of him. Suddenly the front door flew open and Nancy came out with a double barrelled shotgun. Jeb started for her as she raised the gun at Norris.

"Nancy, NOOOO!"

He heard the sharp pop of gunfire. Holes opened up in Nancy's blouse and a chunk of her skull flipped off. His forward motion was now propelled by horror, love and despair. Burning lines tore through his body, his knees buckled as he caught his wife and together they crashed onto the rough-hewn floor. He lay paralyzed, looking at Nancy's upturned face, her eyes empty. It was the last thing he ever saw.

The men reined in their horses, jittery from the gunfire. Through the gun smoke they could see the riddled bodies of the Nortons lying in the doorway. The governor climbed off the buggy.

"Well, that was good target practice." Reece Burton reloaded his pistol, then looked over at Carlos McElroy. "Hey, Carlos, you didn't even draw!"

"I don't shoot women."

Reece shrugged. "All the same to me."

Norris looked at the bodies. "Well, they're dead." He turned to his men. "What happened here today is I paid cash for this ranch and the Nortons decided to go back east."

"Why are we sayin' that, Governor?" Reece protested. "She got what she had comin' for pointin' that shotgun at us."

"Shut up, you idiot. No one would believe some woman would try to take on four gunfighters. The other problem is that if they have kin, they could come and claim the ranch, so just do as I say."

"Sorry, Governor, I guess I wasn't thinkin'."

"I don't pay you to think, Reece."

"Yes, sir."

He pointed to the other two men with him. "You men go get those two horses in the corral and the wagon over there.

"Load these bodies in the wagon then take them a couple of miles away. Make sure you bury them deep to get rid of them. We can't have them showing up later.

"Carlos, you and Reece help me find the Nortons' deed to this ranch. We'll get the signatures forged and have the judge certify the transaction. That way this nice addition to my ranch only cost me the price of the ammunition. That's what I call a good deal!"

Chapter Three

JASPER STARTED EARLY THE NEXT MORNING. He continued along Arlington Creek checking now and again to make sure the gang's trail was still on the road. He checked again at ten miles and saw no sign. Backtracking he spotted where a lone rider met the gang, then they turned west into Tully Valley. The trail appeared to be only a day old. Jasper headed west but took to the high ground, weaving in and out of the tree line.

He rode four hours before he caught a faint whiff of wood smoke. He stopped. A light breeze came from the north with the stronger rushes of air bringing the pleasant smell. He figured the smoke came from the valley north of him. Dismounting, he looped Coal's reins around the saddle horn. He took his Winchester out of the scabbard and pocketed extra cartridges from his saddle bag.

Jasper moved down to the valley slowly so as not to spook the birds and critters around. Any savvy men riding with the outlaws would notice right off if the birds went quiet. His high top moccasins allowed him to glide through the trees without disturbing their soft song.

He reached a rock outcropping and after taking off his hat, Jasper crawled out to take a look see. A group of men and horses gathered around two campfires. The slight breeze carried the wood smoke directly towards him simplifying the aiming calculations for his shots. The men were at least eight hundred yards away. He needed to get closer. A good blanket of trees covered the approach to another outcropping five hundred yards further downhill.

Jasper slid back off the outcropping on his belly. He moved down hill, still slow and quiet, listening for any unnatural sound. His eyes searched the trees like a predator and he felt the grim determination that had set on his face. He neared the second outcropping and went low. Crawling out to the edge, he surveyed the men and the horses. His eyes stopped on a sorrel. He recognized a long hank of blonde hair hanging off the saddle horn. These were the men who killed Claire Dolan. These were the men who killed his pa and his brothers. Yet they seemed not to care about those crimes. Some were eating, some playing a card game, some talking and joking. A hawk cried above them.

The desire to exact justice by death built in Jasper. He planned his shots, gauging how the men would move when he opened fire, as he had done in scores of battles. He knew he wouldn't get them all but he would whittle down their numbers. Patience ruled because he needed to know who might be the owner of the sorrel. He didn't want to kill him...yet. Then he saw it.

One of the men wore an Arkansas Toothpick blade on this left hip. He walked with a swagger around the campfire next to the horses. The man thumped his chest as he strutted over to the sorrel and taking the blonde hair in his right hand, he held the scalp up and let out a war hoop.

Jasper's temples pounded and his jaws clenched. He slid back off the outcropping and rolled over to look up at the sky. Long deep breaths soon replaced fury with cold resolve. He rolled back over and crawled out to the edge.

He pointed his rifle at the man sitting closest to the horses at the nearest fire. Flipping up his rear sight he accounted for wind, adjusted for distance, lined the sights up and placed them on his target. Jasper squeezed the trigger. The rifle boomed and bucked into his shoulder. He smoothly worked the lever, loading another round in the chamber and fired at the next man. This action was repeated six more times and eight men lay on the ground near the horses. Other men ran in various directions seeking cover or a way to escape.

Jasper leveled the rifle again and four more men fell to the ground. Then the camp went quiet. Some managed to get to the horses and rode off. Others were hiding. Dust made it hard for Jasper to see. Sporadic shots came from the valley. Some of the outlaws were shooting blindly, a testament to their inexperience.

He eased off the rock quietly making his way back to Coal and mounted without taking the reins. He gently tapped the horse's flanks. Coal started forward, instinctively following the tree line. Jasper reloaded his Winchester then took the reins guiding the big horse towards the valley at an angle, increasing Coal's speed. He reached a point a thousand yards west of his ambush and three hundred yards from the trail in the valley. Four men rode away in the distance but more horses were coming. Four more men galloped after them from the east. Jasper took aim and fired two shots in quick succession. Now only two riders were galloping away and two lay in the dust, their horses stopped nearby.

Jasper listened, but didn't hear anymore horses. He rode down to the edge of the road and listened again... still nothing. Crossing the road he urged Coal to the trees and headed east, riding slowly, listening and searching the trees for movement.

A stillness settled in the valley and the bright sun warmed the air. A ten minute ride brought Jasper just above the outlaws' campsite. He could see dust in the distance to the east. The birds starting to sing again, an indication no one alive was in the camp and moving. Twelve bodies littered the area but one of them lay moaning and writhing where the horses had been. The others didn't move. He looked across the road to the outcropping from where he did his shooting. Still no movement in the area. He loaded two more rounds into his rifle and dismounted.

He worked his way down to the camp. Starting with the closest man, he checked each body as he moved toward the man who was still alive. The rest were dead.

Jasper walked up to the wounded man. He realized he didn't remember shooting him. The man was young, his holster empty. He held his stomach with his hands, blood seeping through the fingers.

"Help me, mister. I'm gut shot," the man's voice squeezed through his pain.

"I didn't come here to help you."

The man's eyes widened and then he lay back. "Then kill me now. I can't stand this awful hurt."

"Who shot you?"

"That son... of a... bitch... Bart Moore." The young man's words came in short gasps.

"Why?"

"I told him I was... done ridin' with him... just before you started shootin'. After you started... he ran for his horse... but I was in his way."

"Who killed the girl?"

"That... was... Moore's idea. I... didn't want... nothin' to do... with it. It made me... sick to see... what they done."

"Is he the one with the sorrel and the Arkansas Toothpick?"

The young man nodded his head.

"Who shot the old man and the two brothers?"

"Moore and... several... others. One of them finished off the old man and the younger one. I didn't... like that... either."

"Why'd you ride with these men?"

"I got no kin and... nowhere to go. They... kinda took... me in."

"Where's Moore from?"

"Kentville."

Jasper bent down and moved the young man's hands. He'd seen many wounds like it during the War Between the States. "That wound's goin' to kill you, boy. Ain't no doctorin' goin' to fix it."

The young man took a deep, painful breath. "Just... finish me. Please, mister... I can't take it no more."

Jasper rose and stepped back and drew a Colt. He pointed it and the young man nodded, turning his eyes to the sky. Jasper could clearly see the pimples on the kid's face and the scraggly thin beard starting to grow. He shook his head. "May God accept your soul."

Bart Moore galloped towards Arlington Road with five of his men. After two miles Moore started slowing his horse down. The others followed his lead. Moore turned in his saddle and looked over their back trail.

"I don't see no dust back there. I don't think anyone is chasin' us."

"Who the hell was doin' all that shootin'?" Dewey Cann wondered aloud.

"I don't know," Moore replied quietly. He looked back again.

"I hope it wasn't Jasper Lee," Harry Wells mused. "Arlington is his territory and whoever did that shootin' was as good as Lee."

"All right, you shit heads. It don't do no good wonderin'. We don't even know how many shooters were there. We need to keep movin'."

"Don't you think you'd better get rid of that scalp, Bart?" Cann asked.

Moore felt the thick golden blonde hair hanging off his saddle horn. "Hell no! I'm going to make me somethin' out of this hair so's I can remember how good it felt to have her squirmin' under me while I cut her. I must a come ten times!" Moore laughed hard and loud as he spurred his horse down the road.

Moore's laugh sent a shiver up Harry Wells' spine, same as a sidewinder's rattle would. He spit out his wad of tobacco. "Crazy son of a bitch!" He said out loud.

"What'd you say?" Cann asked.

"I said Moore's a crazy son of a bitch."

"Watch what you say about my friend, Wells."

"Sure, Dewey. Let's ride."

Chapter Four

WHEN JOHNNY STEWART AND RICH DELTON stumbled into the Oak Tree Saloon in Lowell Town, cowboy Sandy James noticed they were dirty, tired...and their eyes were filled with fear. He also noticed dried blood on their pants. He started to return to his conversation with his friends when his attention was drawn by the word "ambush."

Sandy turned to the bar. "You say something about an ambush?"

"What's it to ya?" Stewart sneered.

"I was only asking because we got word of a posse being ambushed a couple of days ago."

Stewart's eyes darted around and Delton looked down at the bar and put his face in his glass of beer.

"Don't know nothin' about a posse. *We* was ambushed!"

"Well, it looks like you came out of it all right."

"We did, but a lot of our friends didn't."

"What happened?"

"We was just camped out when someone opened up on us from the side of the mountain. Killed at least eight or ten of our friends in less than half a minute."

Sandy's interest grew. "Hadn't you boys better report this to the town marshal?"

Stewart spun around and gave Sandy a hard look. "Why don't you mind your own business."

"There's only one man I know that can kill ten men in less than half a minute."

"Yeah, who's that?"

"Jasper Lee. I rode with him for a year back in the cattle wars. He don't kill men unless they need killin'."

Everyone in the saloon looked at Stewart and Delton. Stewart's face turned pale at the mention of Jasper's name. Rich Delton's knuckles turned white as his hand tightened around the handle on his glass.

"Word is someone shot down Jasper's pa and brothers and kidnapped a girl," Sandy continued. "Wouldn't know anything about that would you?"

Stewart put his hand on his gun. "I'm goin' to tell you for the last time...mind your own damn business!"

A heavy silence descended upon the room except for the wind whispering at the swinging doors. Sandy looked over to see Jasper Lee standing just inside, the sun through the opening casting his long shadow on the sawdust covered floor. Jasper looked the saloon over. Sandy had seen the look on Jasper's face before and a shudder went through him.

Jasper nodded to Sandy and then focused on Stewart and Delton. "There's two horses outside that've been rode hard. Who do they belong to?" He looked at Stewart and Delton, taking in their appearance, especially the dried blood...Claire's blood.

"They belong to you men?"

"What are ya goin' to do about it?" Stewart growled.

Jasper spoke in a deep, calm voice. "You men killed my pa and my brothers. Then you raped and killed Claire Dolan. For those crimes, I'm goin' to kill you."

Two men rose from their table and walked over to stand with Stewart and Delton. "We're standing with these men. We fought agin you during the cattle wars, Lee. We figure we owe you a couple of bullets."

"You heard what they did. You stand with them...you die with 'em."

Sandy stood, but Jasper waved him away.

Johnny Stewart pulled on his gun.

Jasper sprung to the right. By the time he reached the cover of the bar his Long Colt .45 had spit flame and lead twice.

Before Johnny Stewart could raise his gun to shoot his back erupted with blood and flesh. He collapsed to the ground like a sack of potatoes.

The man who challenged Jasper joined Stewart in death as Jasper's next bullets slammed into his heart and gut before his gun cleared his holster. The man fell backwards, his head bouncing off the floor.

Rich Delton didn't even draw but ducked behind the other end of the bar.

The last man fired one wild shot at Jasper and ran for the rear door. Jasper shot him in the back, the bullets lifting the man off his feet, smashing him into the wall where he crumpled into the sawdust on the floor.

The saloon was filled with dust and gun smoke. The acrid smell of burnt gunpowder hung with a moment of reverberating gunfire. It was replaced with an eerie silence, laced with the whimpering of Rich Delton. He threw his gun out on the floor in front of the bar. "I don't want no fight, Mr. Lee. Please don't kill me!"

"Did you kill my pa and brothers?" Jasper drew his other Colt and stuck the empty one in his belt, which he reloaded with his left hand while covering Delton with his other pistol.

Delton didn't answer right away. Then he said, "Yes," in the form of a sob. "I shot one of your brothers...but I wasn't the only one. I don't know if my shot killed him."

"Did you rape Claire Dolan?"

"Oh, God!" Delton moaned. He was crying loudly now. "I had a turn with her, but almost everyone else did too. But I had nothin' to do with killin' her. That was all Bart Moore. He went crazy over her and just kept cuttin' away with his knife. It made me sick, Mr. Lee, honest."

"Tell me why I shouldn't kill you."

"Because he's under arrest," another voice interrupted. "And you'll be too if you don't holster that gun."

Jasper looked over his shoulder and saw Stan Barstow, the Lowell Town Marshal, gun in hand. "I got no quarrel with you, Marshal, but I guess you heard what he said. Natural law demands I kill him."

"In this town the law of the territory is followed. He'll be brought to justice for his crimes. Now get both those guns into their holsters."

Jasper slowly rose from behind the bar and put his guns away. Frustration worked his gut.

The marshal walked over to the other end of the bar and picked Delton up by the collar. "You're under arrest, Rich Delton, for kidnapping, rape and murder." The marshal locked a set of manacles on Delton's wrists. "Please follow me to the jail, Mr. Lee. I'll need a statement from you."

Sandy James approached the marshal. "I saw the whole thing, Marshal. The three men Jasper shot all drew on him first...he was just a lot faster."

The marshal nodded. "You come too and give a statement."

After Jasper and Sandy had given their statements, the marshal had some advice for Jasper.

"Mr. Lee, Delton identified everyone involved in the killing of your kin and the rape and murder of the girl. I'll be sending a report to the county prosecutor. I expect he'll have warrants issued shortly. You best leave this to the law to handle."

"Thanks for your work, Marshal."

"And one more thing. I'm not doin' much about the shooting in Tully Valley Delton told me about, just because he can't say who did it. The location is out of my jurisdiction too. But I'd tread carefully if I were you. This man, Bart Moore, is kin to the governor of this territory. Nephew, I think. You didn't hear this from me but the governor isn't exactly an honest politician, if there is such a thing. In fact, he may just be one of the worst."

"I appreciate your concern. Marshal, I'd be obliged if'n you sent a message home that I buried Claire Dolan near where the posse was ambushed, in the boulders across from Arlington Creek. I gave her a decent burial in a nice area. It's up to the family, but tell 'em it'd be better to leave her rest there. "

"I'll take care of it."

Jasper and Sandy left the marshal's office and headed over to Kate's Cafe for dinner.

"What you goin' to do now, Jasper, head for Kentville?"

"No, I saw the trail of four riders who ran before Stewart and Delton, heading northwest. I'm goin' to pick up that trail."

"You'll be headin' into Indian country!"

Jasper nodded. "I got no quarrel with the clan."

"Yeah, but they might not feel the same."

"I have friends there."

"Black Feather?"

"He's a good friend."

"Maybe. I think you're the only white man he ever respected, but I ain't sure he counts you as his friend."

Jasper emptied his cup. "He does."

Sandy looked at Jasper and shook his head. "If'n you say so."

Chapter Five

GALE PULLED HARD on the rope attached to the bucket, hand over hand, drawing water from the well. It was apt for her name to be spelled like a storm. Her fiery red hair matched her temperament. The well sat in the middle of the ranch yard behind the house, with the large barn and corrals on one side and the chicken coup and pig sty on the other. Three mares and four geldings stood in the corrals, some hens made their bok-bok and screech as they bobbed around the coop, a large red rooster lording over them. Black and white spotted pigs slept in the mud to protect themselves from the mid-morning sun.

"Brenden, you get over here young man!"

Twelve year old Brenden slumped in submission and walked over to his mother.

"Just because your pa's gone for a while don't mean you can shirk your chores. You get to cleanin' out the barn b'fore I tan your backside like a cow's hide."

"Oh, Ma, I should'a gone with pa. He needs me to help him kill those men who killed grandpa."

Gale grabbed her son by the shoulders, the water bucket left to plummet to the depths of the well. The tears streaming down her cheeks only stoked the fire in her heart.

"You listen to me, Brenden Lee. It's bad enough I've got to worry about your pa gone three days with no word! I won't let you run off with a gun in your hand and drive me crazy waitin' for you to come home in a wooden box, too."

Brenden looked into his mother's eyes and squeezed her shoulder. "I'm sorry, Ma. I'll get the barn done." He went to the barn, looking back and forcing a smile before he went in.

Gale slowly sat down on the well wall, holding her face in her hands, her worry over Jasper bursting the dam of the brave face she tried to put on, unleashing a river of tears.

"Pa will be all right, Ma. There's nobody stronger or tougher than him."

Gale looked into the gentle blue eyes of her daughter, Megan. Younger Abbey stood behind her. Gale pulled them into her arms, kissing them on the cheek. "Thank the Lord I have you two and your brothers."

"We love you, Ma."

Gale gave her daughters a squeeze and then stood, straightening her split gingham skirt. She looked at the bucket rope, sighed, and then started pulling up water again."

"Hello, the ranch!" Gale recognized Micah Niles' voice. She turned to see Burt Ashton with him. She wrapped the rope around a stay bar. "Hello, gentlemen, what brings you here?"

"Mornin', Gale," Micah greeted her. "Jasper asked us to check on you every now and again, to see if we could help you at all."

Gale wiped her forehead with the back of her hand. "That's neighborly of you. If you have the time I'd appreciate if you'd ride out and help Sean check on our herd. I haven't been able to get out there for a couple of days."

"We'll do that. Do you have any heavy liftin' that needs doin'?"

"I believe the boys and I can handle most of the liftin' around here."

"All right then. We'll head out to the herd."

"Thank you, kindly."

"One more thing, Gale. There's a meetin' in town tomorrow about appointin' a new sheriff until we can hold an election. You should consider being there."

"I got no interest in political things."

"There's talk of appointin' Jasper as sheriff. You might want to come and give some idea on what he would think about that."

Gale stood stunned and silent for a good minute before words found their way out of her mouth. "I'll give some thought to it, Micah."

The men tipped their hats and rode out toward the summer range of the Lee ranch.

"Gale Lee is quite a handsome woman," Burt Ashton observed as he scratched his bushy beard.

Micah chuckled. "I've known Gale since we was kids. She is indeed a handsome woman, if you like hurricanes."

"So, she's strong willed I take it."

"I'll say Jasper Lee is just about the only man I believe could handle her and I estimate it's just barely."

Burt smiled and shook his head. "Better him than me."

Micah looked at his friend. "I reckon so."

They rode in silence for awhile enjoying the new warmth and the fragrance of the pine and wild roses brought by spring.

"They certainly have made this into a fine ranch," Burt observed.

"Well, they work hard and Jasper is a fair and shrewd businessman. I don't know anyone who won't do business with him. I've been involved with some deals with him and I can say we both made very good money."

"How did you come to do business with him?"

"I wanted to take a herd to market and I wanted someone I could trust with me on the drive. Well, Jasper was takin' his herd to market at the same time, so we joined up. He'd already studied the market and knew what beef was goin' for in Chicago, so when we got down to sellin' the cattle he negotiated a damn good price. So now, we always go together."

"How did he know the price in Chicago?"

"He has a friend from his Army days who sends him the price by telegraph. Jasper gets the price before the market here does."

"He is indeed a shrewd man."

"He is and has been a good friend to me."

"An interesting man for a gunfighter."

"I wouldn't call him a gunfighter. I'd call him a man who fights for the things he believes in."

Sean Lee had spent the last ten minutes using his Bowie knife to cut a bawling calf out of tangled brush. He got most of it cut away in front of the calf and slapped its hind quarter with his hat. The calf jumped, freeing himself and running off to his mother. Sean smiled.

He mounted his horse, taking a deep breath of mountain spring air. He scanned around him and saw two riders coming toward him in the distance. He pulled his Winchester out of the scabbard, resting the butt of the stock on his thigh to show he was armed. The men still came on.

Sean lowered the rifle to the crook of his arm, levered a round into the chamber and at the ready until he recognized Micah Niles and Burt Ashton. He lowered the hammer and put the rifle back in the scabbard.

"Not takin' any chances are you, Sean." Micah pulled his horse to a stop.

"Not since Grandpa and my uncles were murdered, Mr. Niles."

"Can't say I blame you. Your Ma asked us to help you check on the herd."

"I appreciate that. I need to get over to Grandpa's place and check the herd there. I only have this hill in back of me left to check for any of the herd that may be stuck in the brush. If we can spread out and work it, we can get it done in no time at all."

"Let's do her," Burt said.

"I'll take the top," Sean offered and started up the hill. When he reached the top, he cut right and leaned forward in the saddle so he could look over the tall brush. He was thankful for the cowhide chaps protecting his legs.

It only took twenty minutes to clear the hill and roust four head of cattle along with two covey of quail. Sean joined the others at the bottom of the hill.

"Thank you, Mr. Niles and Mr. Ashton. I appreciate it."

"Glad to help, Sean. Your herd is lookin' good."

"Yes, sir, it is. The summer feedin' should make them filled out enough to bring a handsome price at the market."

"You drivin' with your pa again this year?"

"Oh, yes, sir."

"Good. It's always good to have you along, Sean. You're a top hand."

"Thank you, Mr. Niles. I best be gettin' to Grandpa's."

"Need any help there?"

"No, sir. I cleared it two days ago. I'm just doing a check today."

Micah nodded. "We'll see you later."

Micah and Burt started back for their homes.

"That boy is the spittin' image of his pa," Burt observed.

"That's a fact and in more ways than looks. He was a hard workin' cowboy on the cattle drive last year. Jasper took a lot of time to teach him the ways of the trail…and of men."

"I hope he tempered his view of men a bit."

Micah laughed. "Not likely. Sean will grow up to be as good a man as Jasper…probably just as hard."

"I don't think that's good for a boy. The world is a changin' and hard men won't be welcome in time."

"Maybe, because a lot of folks are fearful of a man who ain't afraid. But I think bad men will always be around and hard men will always be needed to rein 'em in."

Burt nodded. "Ya got a point there, but I'll bet Gale don't like what Sean's learnin'. No mother would."

"That's probably true. I imagine she's worried enough about Jasper and she'll definitely worry about Sean if he straps on six-guns."

"Well, let's hope it don't get to that."

"More than likely it will."

Chapter Six

JASPER RODE FOR TWO HOURS before he crossed into Indian country. He started before sunrise as he knew he had to make up some time. Sandy tried to come along with him but Jasper insisted he could take care of these four by himself. He followed their trail with no trouble. The tracks showed they had ridden their horses into the ground and they had to dismount for a time. Jasper smiled to himself. He learned many years ago that getting too much in a hurry causes more trouble than any hurrying is worth.

An hour later he came on Indian Jack's place. Jack was a cantankerous old man, half-Indian, with three daughters. His wife had long ago gone to the spirit world. He ran a herd of horses he pulled wild off the open range and broke to sell. He also ran a herd of cattle he populated with range cows and a little rustling here and there. The trail of the four men led to Jack's ramshackle house.

Jasper spent ten minutes looking the area over from a hill to the east of the ranch house. The morning was bright and cool. Jack's ranch sat in a saddle of land surrounded by deep green mountain grass and capped with tree lined foothills. Jasper's eyes searched every visible nook and corner. A few cows grazed near the back of the house, but a bad feeling snaked through his gut when he saw the corral gate wide open with no horses inside. Nothing moved, except cow tails swatting flies, so he started for the house. The only sounds were the thump of Coal's hooves and the creak of saddle leather. A cow lifted her spotted head and mooed when Jasper reined Coal to a stop.

"Easy, Bessie. It's just me." Jasper knew the cows were disturbed by the same smell his nostrils caught...the smell of decomposing flesh. He stood on his stirrups and saw a thick patch of flies just past a stack of hay. Jack's body lay in a crumpled heap just on the other side.

Jasper hit the ground fast and hurried over to Jack. He had been dead for at least a day, maggots already doing their work. Jasper stopped counting bullet holes when he got to ten. Drawing a Colt he went to the front door of the house.

"Hello, the house!"

No answer.

He kicked the door open, then quickly moved off to the right. He looked into the main room from there, then crossed over to check from the left before he stepped inside.

The kitchen table was flipped on its side. Jasper picked up the leg that had broken off. Two wooden chairs and a stool lay smashed next to the wall separating the living area from the bedrooms. Pieces of crockery were strewn everywhere. A torn woman's shirt straddled the door that led to the sleeping room. Inside he discovered a skirt that had been ripped from waist to hem and a hand woven blanket on one of the beds had a good sized stain on it, the brownish-red color of dried blood. There were no other bodies. Jasper hoped Jack's daughters had been able to escape but he figured the men had probably kidnapped them.

He went back outside and set to the task of preparing Indian Jack for the spirit world. He found the best of Jack's clothes he could, clean buckskin pants and a buckskin shirt with a breast plate of red and blue beads forming the Circle of Life. Bands of matching beads circled the cuffs.

After washing Jack's body, Jasper dressed the old man. Then he found Jack's best blanket, one made by his wife before she died and wrapped him in it, except for his head, so he could see the spirits when they came to lead him to the campfires in the sky. Jasper did the spirit dance around Jack's body, chanting, calling the spirits to come so they might grant him passage into the spirit world. Then he carried Jack to the large oak tree in front of the house and laid him in the crook of the tree so the spirits would find him.

When he finished, Jasper mounted Coal and continued on the trail until the sun sought the horizon. Angling up an incline to a rock face, he stopped at a shallow cave at the foot of the cliff. He dismounted and set up camp. Then he brushed, fed and watered Coal.

Later, Jasper sipped coffee, watching the sun disappear in the cooling air fragrant with pine and juniper. Shafts of light came through the fading clouds and splashed muted orange, blue and purple hues onto the hills and cliffs, bringing colored memories of his pa and younger brothers. A heaviness descended upon him. His breaking heart urged a flow of tears past his resolve. The faces of his kin were there with him in the darkness, but they were soon replaced by the face of the wounded young man looking skyward. The memory unsettled Jasper's spirit as if a rift cracked the truth of his universe. He could see the young man's eyes again but now they were filled with hurt, abandonment, and an unanswered question.

When the moon had risen high Jasper heard his brother, Black Feather, come into the camp. He stirred the fire to get more warmth then spread his saddle blanket and laid down close by. Jasper felt at peace and slipped back into sleep.

"Mornin', brother," Jasper said as he squinted into the morning sun, a little embarrassed his brother rose before him.

"Good Morning, Fire Hawk. I have made coffee," Black Feather offered.

"Ah, it smells good."

"I've heard the news of the death of our father and brothers. My heart hurts."

"It's a hard thing."

"I am filled with the memories of father's warm heart and the love of our brothers. They accepted me as family as soon as *we* became brothers."

"As your family did me."

"We have come through many good summers and some hard winters."

"And we still remain brothers."

"That will be for all time, Fire Hawk. You are looking for the men who killed them." Black Feather was making a statement, not asking a question.

"I've found many of them but four rode here. They went to Indian Jack's ranch, stole his horses and killed him. They took his daughters, too."

"We found his daughters and the men who killed Jack."

Jasper looked at Black Feather. "How are the daughters?"

"Soft Rain is dead. Moon On The Water and Butterfly Wing were violated and tortured. They are ruined."

Jasper looked at the ground. He loved his brother and his people, but their attitude towards raped women bothered him. "Will you ban them and send them into the wilderness?"

"It is our way. We will banish them after they have their justice, as you say."

"I'll take them with me."

Black Feather considered his brother's statement. "Will you take them as wives?"

"You know I have a wife. One is enough. I'll employ them until they decide what they want to do. I have to care for our father's ranch now, too. They'll be a great help."

"Maybe that might be good, but they are Jack's daughters and like him in many ways."

"I know, but remember who I'm married to. I can handle them."

Black Feather laughed. "I guess you like trouble because there's no trouble like a strong-minded woman and you are talking about adding two more!"

"What about the men?"

Black Feather's face turned to stone. "We killed one. We have the others. I was riding to check on Jack so I can relate their full crime to the council lodge."

"Jack was shot many times. I asked the spirits to take him according to custom."

"Thank you, brother. After we eat we'll ride to our village."

The two men rode slowly, recounting their younger days and remembering their happiness with Pa and the brothers. They talked of the hunting, fishing trips and campfires they all shared. Black

Feather told of the contest he and the brothers had to see who could swing the farthest onto the river with a rope that hung on a giant oak next to the bank.

"I remember Caleb trying to swing out, but he was so young and skinny, he couldn't get enough movement from the rope. He wouldn't give up, swinging time after time until his arms and hands failed him. Though not strong in his body, Caleb's heart had the strength of a bear."

Jasper heard Black Feather swallow hard and looked over to see rivulets of tears. They rode the rest of the way in companionable silence.

Bart Moore sat on his horse just outside the Kentville town limits. One of the governor's men came by the gang's cabin and told Bart his uncle wanted to see him. When Bart asked what his uncle wanted, the man only answered the governor wasn't happy about something.

The nervous stomping of the hooves of his horse echoed the churning in Bart's gut. He always felt like a failure in his uncle eyes. Uncle Cornell was a no-nonsense man. At times he could be downright mean. Those times brought back the awful ghost of his father.

The memory of his father drove his emotions to the highest levels and to the lowest like a demented yo-yo. Bart winced at the thought of the beatings his father used to give him in his early years. The words his father spewed out as his arm swung the strap up and down hurt nearly as much as the beating. But when he turned eleven, his father took an interest in him. Taught him how to cheat at cards, how to drink, how to steal, how to shoot and other things his father said were useful in life. Getting this attention and to be liked by his father thrilled young Bart…until he turned thirteen.

On the night of his thirteenth birthday he shared a hotel room with his father on Bourbon Street. Father took him for a steak dinner and bought him his first drink. In the steamy, hot New Orleans night, a drowsy Bart stripped off his clothes and drifted off thinking his life was going turn out okay. He woke from a hazy sleep when his father and another man came into the room. Both men were drunk. His father lit a lamp while the other man yanked off the sheet and Bart jumped up, embarrassed and trying to cover his privates.

The stranger gave Bart a good looking over. "Yeah, he'll do nicely." He handed Bart's father a wad of money.

Both men came towards him.

Bart instinctively backed away, but they grabbed him and pushed him onto the bed. His father held him down while the other man pulled his hips up and got in between his legs.

"Pap, don't let him hurt me!"

"It's okay, Bart. Just relax. You'll get twenty bucks when this is over."

Bart started to scream as the man pushed himself into Bart's bunghole, but his father covered his mouth. Bart gritted his teeth while tears poured from his eyes in anger, humiliation and betrayal. Time went gone to the end of the universe and back before the man finally satisfied himself.

Tortured relief swept through Bart now that no more hands touched him. He was hurt, but he turned to look at his father and the man talking quietly. A rampant fury filled his chest. He pulled the Arkansas Toothpick he kept under his pillow for protection, sprang from the bed and drove the knife into his father's back. At the same time he pulled his father's pistol.

His rapist was slow to react and Bart shot him twice in the chest. The man dropped in a heap.

Bart walked to the rapist and their eyes met. Bart shot him in the crotch, then watched blood soak through the cloth and start to cover the floor like an incoming tide.

He turned to his father, who squirmed on the floor trying to reach the knife in his back. "You sold me, you son of a bitch." Bart aimed the gun and shot his father twice in the face. He stood for a long moment staring at his father's mangled visage.

Yelling outside and banging on the door jacked him out of his haze. Grabbing his clothes and the bloodstained wad of bills the rapist had given his father, he climbed out of the window. Making his way along a series of roofs he found a drain pipe and shimmied down, collapsing in an alley from the pain in his bunghole. He knew he was bleeding but nothing could be done about it at the moment. He crawled to a stack of barrels, hiding behind them while he dressed. He eventually made it to a Creole witch who fixed him up with surprising compassion. He decided to let her live.

Then he headed West to look for his mother. He knew her brother took her to one of the territories when Bart and his father left her. He also knew his uncle was some kind of big shot. It took a while, but he found them.

The coming meeting with his uncle whisked the memory away. His uncle, the governor of the territory, was the most powerful and important man he had ever known. He desperately wanted the man to like him. Bart steeled himself, half- heartedly spurring his horse to trot down the ridge to the governor's office. He stopped in front of one of the governor's men.

"'Bout time you got here," the man said as Moore climbed the steps to the porch. "The ol' man is like a caged mountain lion."

Bart swallowed hard and stepped through the door.

"Get in here, Bart!" His uncle called from across the foyer.

Bart walked into the office.

"Close the door."

He pushed the door shut.

"What in the hell have you done?"

An endless list of crimes flashed through his mind. "I ain't done nothin'," Bart sputtered.

"Nothing! You call murder and rape 'nothing'!"

"There ain't no proof I done such things."

The governor grabbed papers off his desk. "No? How about a statement from an outlaw by the name of Rich Delton who says he was there and it was all your idea. The Cassidy County judge is considering issuing a warrant for your arrest. "

Bart felt blood draining from his face but his mouth sneered. "Rich Delton is an idiot and liar."

"Oh, really? And just how do you know this Rich Delton?"

Bart swallowed the lump in his throat but made no reply.

"Damn, if you weren't my sister's son I'd hang you myself."

"Uncle…"

"Shut up! If you want to live, you listen to me and do exactly as I say." Uncle Cornell handed him a map. "You go out to my ranch and get a bed at the bunk house. Tell the new foreman I said to hire you on. Tell 'em your name is John Smith. You work and stay on that ranch until I tell you to move. You don't say anything except 'yes, sir,' 'no, sir,' and 'thank you, sir.' You got it?"

"Yes, sir."

"You better because word is Jasper Lee is looking for you. The men you killed were his father and brothers."

A jolt of fear shot through Bart's spine.

"He shot a Johnny Stewart and two other cowboys," Uncle Cornell continued. "He would've killed Delton, too, but the Lowell Town marshal stopped him."

Bart stood mute, fumbling with his hat. "Get out of here!" The governor growled.

The ride back to the cabin left plenty of time for fear to smolder into anger and anger to flame into loathing.

He's upset over a rape?! No one gave a damn about me getting raped! And murder...he has no idea how many trusting idiots I've killed. Bart straightened himself in the saddle and pushed his chest out. *I've left bodies from New Orleans to here. I took everything they owned and no one knows...no one knows. Those three men and the girl were nothin'. If that old son of a bitch don't watch it, I'll show him who's the most powerful man around here!*

He dug his spurs into his horse and galloped to the cabin.

Cornell Norris sat at his desk twirling a pencil as he contemplated the acts of his nephew. He worried about the affect they may have on his goals.

He'd sacrificed, risked, fought, cheated and killed to get control of everything around him...the land, the money, the governorship...and then there's Bart...a crazy, uncontrollable liability.

Cornell loved his sister. If she hadn't protected him when they were kids, he would've ended up as bad as Bart. But she did protect him and she paid hell for it. He couldn't forget that...wouldn't forget it, no matter what. *We deserve better than what we got as kids and I'm going to see we get it.*

Cornell figured when he became senator he'd have enough money to woo the most politically connected single woman in Washington D.C. and start building his political base to make a run for president. When he became president nothing could stop him from becoming the richest and most powerful man in the country.

... but Bart may just be too much of a problem.

The description of the murders in the report, especially the murder of the girl, were just too horrendous. If word got out connecting Bart to those deaths, it would ruin Cornell. Ruin any chance of him being a US Senator. Ruin any chance of wooing a politically connected woman. Ruin any chance at giving his sister a better life. He would do whatever he needed to do to keep a lid on this.

Chapter Seven

MOST ALL OF THE RESIDENTS of Cassidy County attended the meeting to appoint a new sheriff. Micah looked around for Gale but she wasn't there. He hoped she would come to the meeting and approve of Jasper's appointment. Micah knew only Gale could convince Jasper to accept.

"Quiet down! Quiet down! This here meetin' will come to order!" Bill Newlin, the chairman of the county commission called out.

An unsettled quiet filled the room.

"Okay, thank you. We're here today to appoint a new sheriff. This appointment will be temporary until we hold an election. Because of the urgency of the situation we're going to take nominations from the group here today and the commissioners will appoint one of those nominated."

The door opened and Micah turned to see if his hope had been fulfilled. Gale stepped inside.

He rose to his feet. "Mr. Chairman, I have a nomination."

"Go ahead, Micah."

"I nominate Jasper Lee."

The room filled with murmurs and muffled exclamations.

"Order! Order! Is Jasper here?" Bill asked.

"No, he ain't," someone said.

"Well, I don't think it's right to nominate someone who ain't here," Bill commented. "He can't speak for himself."

"I can speak for him," Gale almost whispered.

"Wait a minute!" Horace Baily called out. "Jasper Lee is a violent man and a known killer. We can't have him as sheriff!"

Micah could feel the blood flush to his face. "Horace, you weren't here during the cattle wars. All you've heard about Jasper is part rumor and part legend. Jasper fought in the War Between the States and came back a decorated cavalry officer. He found his family's ranches, and those of his neighbors, in jeopardy from marauding ex-soldiers from both sides who raided ranches, committing murder and rape, while stealing ranch lands and cattle. He organized the ranchers to fight back. That's how the cattle wars began. They lasted for seven months, off and on. The wars ended largely because of Jasper's pursuit of the criminals and his reputation for no quarter frightened most of them off."

"That's the part I don't understand. I hear tell he killed more men than was needed."

"Depends on your point of view. In my opinion, Jasper did what he had to do. We all did for that matter."

"Well, I hope it don't happen again."

Micah didn't answer right away as several unpleasant pictures flew through his mind. Then a long breath escaped through his teeth. "We can always hope. Jasper is the only one among us who had the guts to go after the killers who committed the worst crime in this county for a long time. From all accounts, he's taking care of business we all should be doin'. You got no right sayin' he's a bad man."

Horace pointed his finger at Micah. "That don't mean..."

"My husband is *not* a bad man!" Gale's voice rang clear and true. "He can be a hard man, I'll give you that, but this is hard country. Times come when we have need of hard men.

"There's not a person in this room that can call Jasper a cheat, a fraud, or a thief. When many of you needed help, he came to you. I can't recall a time when he turned down any one of you that asked for his help and there's that many again that he helped without your asking. Landsakes, Horace, when you took sick he worked day and night on both our ranches until you got well! If it hadn't been for him, you'd a lost your ranch. And now you say bad things about him! Not a one of you can say Jasper's not a man of his word and y'all know if he's appointed sheriff, he'll be fair and honest."

Jessica Dolan, Claire's mother, stood. "We received word from the marshal in Lowell Town that Jasper found and buried Claire. I went to her grave. Jasper was careful to make it a fitting resting place for our beautiful girl. A bad man doesn't do things like that. As you all know my husband's wounds prevent him from being here but he urges the commission to appoint Jasper as the sheriff of this county."

"Do ya think he'd accept the appointment, Gale?" Bill asked.

"I don't rightly know. He has his own thoughts about the law and justice. But if you appoint him, I'll talk to him. No promises, mind you, but I'll speak my piece."

"Mr. Chairman," Micah called. "It's my suggestion, unless there's other nominations, you appoint Jasper Lee, Sheriff of Cassidy County startin' back when Carl Williams was killed. He's already brought several of those criminals to justice. I believe he should have our blessing for what he's done and for his hunt for the rest of them."

The chairman looked around the room. "Are there any other nominations?"

No one spoke.

The chairman smacked his gavel on the table. "The nominations are closed. Those commissioners in favor of appointing Jasper Lee as Sheriff of Cassidy County, say aye."

The vote was unanimous.

"Those commissioners in favor of allowing Gale Lee to accept the appointment on behalf of Jasper Lee, say aye."

The vote was unanimous again.

"Is this legal?" someone shouted.

"How in the heck do I know?" Bill answered. "I ain't no lawyer, but we don't have the time to dicker. Until further notice, Jasper Lee is the sheriff of this county and that's that."

The chairman waved and after a deep breath to steady herself, Gale walked forward. She held her head high and was happy she wore a dress so no one could see her shaking knees.

She stood in front of the council. She wasn't nervous about the people in the meeting, but thoughts about Jasper's reaction made her heart pound like a horse's galloping hooves.

"Gale Lee, do you firmly believe Jasper Lee will accept this appointment?"

"Yes." *After I talk to him.*

The Chairman nodded. "Please raise your right hand. Does Jasper Lee solemnly swear to defend and uphold the Constitution of the United States and enforce its laws and the laws of this territory?"

"He does."

"I hereby appoint Jasper Lee Sheriff of Cassidy County as of the death of Sheriff Carl Williams." He handed Gale the sheriff's badge and banged the gavel. "This meetin' is adjourned."

Gale stood still, looking at the badge in her hand. *Lord, what have I done.* Memories of Jasper's comments about law and justice percolated through her mind. She closed her fingers around the badge, swallowing hard.

A hand fell gently on her shoulder. "You all right, Gale?"

She turned and looked at Micah. "I think I've created the greatest test of Jasper's love I could ever conceive."

"I don't think anything could shake his love for you. Until this tragedy he's stayed close to home, workin' hard for you and the kids."

"I know. I don't want to lose that."

"Have faith, Gale. He's a good man. He'll do the right thing."

She hurried out the door, tears fell from her eyes. She could only hope Micah was right.

Bart Moore dismounted at the broken down cabin where the last five of his men were hiding. The cabin was back in the trees a ways from the confluence of the Seneca River and Big Muddy Creek. Aside from the sound of the wind in the trees and critters going about their day, the colliding waters made a constant low rumbling undertone.

"What's the news, Bart?" Dewey Cann asked.

"It was Jasper Lee who ambushed us. After the ambush he tracked down Johnny Stewart and Rich Delton. He shot Johnny in a saloon in Lowell Town along with two cowboys." The Lowell Town Marshal saved Delton but he's in jail now."

"Shit, Bart, what are we goin' to do? Jasper Lee is a natural born killer. We don't stand a chance against him."

"Don't give me any of your goddamn whinin', Dewey! I ain't afraid of Jasper Lee."

"Well, you'd better be," Harry Wells said after spitting a short stream of tobacco juice. "I know Lee and he's a curly wolf. Fought with him during the War Between the States and agin' him in the Cattle Wars. He's fearless and the best fightin' man I've ever seen."

"You sound like you like the son-of-a-bitch, Wells."

"I don't necessarily like him, but I do respect him."

Bart looked at Harry. His thoughts lingered on the word *respect* and the anger started to boil inside him again. His hand rested on the butt of his pistol. "I'm just as dangerous as Jasper Lee, Harry. How come you don't respect me like you do him?"

"Didn't say I don't, Bart. I'm just tellin' you that Jasper is nobody to take lightly."

Bart relaxed a little, satisfied he had put Harry in his place. "Well, we ain't goin' to have to fight him. My uncle's takin' care of business. We just gotta lay low until he gets things set straight. I gotta go to his ranch for a while. You boys stay here until you hear from me." Bart mounted and jerked the reins to point his horse in the opposite direction. "And don't cause no trouble!"

Harry Wells picked up his saddle and blanket and walked over to his horse.

"Where the hell do you think you're goin'?" Dewey Cann asked.

"Like I told you before, that Bart Moore is crazy. I ain't waitin' around for him. I'm gettin' outta this territory."

"He told us to stay here."

Wells finished saddling his horse and mounted. "Look around you, Dewey. Moore's goin' to a nice comfortable ranch while he wants us to stay out in this dump. Does that make any sense to you?"

"He says his uncle is going to straighten things out."

"His uncle is a no good lyin', cheatin' politican. I don't trust either of 'em. Good luck to all of you." Wells turned his horse and started toward the trail.

Cann waited a few seconds before he drew his pistol and fired. Wells slumped forward in his saddle, but his horse galloped off.

"Shall we go finish him off?" Jackson Smith asked.

"Hell no!" Cann holstered his pistol. "I shot him didn't I?"

"Well, sure you did."

"Well then he's dead because I don't miss."

Gale stepped outside into the fading sun. Shading her eyes, she looked around and spotted a lone rider heading towards the ranch house. He rode with the butt of a Winchester resting on his thigh. Sean was coming in later than usual. She let out a long sigh as he approached. Both pride and dread filled her heart at the sight of her son riding like a strong man, but he seemed too comfortable with the rifle for her liking.

"Hello, Ma."

"You stayed out much later than usual."

A sly smile crossed Sean's face. "You worried about me meeting some pretty face out here, Ma?"

"Don't get smart with me, young man." Gale was smiling, but the word *man* caught in her throat.

Sean slipped the Winchester in its scabbard, dismounted and gave his mother a hug. "Just following Pa's evening track and makin' sure everything is well."

Gale put her hand on Sean's cheek and felt the beginnings of a beard. Thank you, son, but what took you so long?"

"Pa taught me that when I ride perimeter not to leave any question unanswered."

"I don't understand."

"Pa says we all see things that raise questions in our mind but we ignore most of them. When you ride perimeter you don't ignore any of them. Other soldiers' lives depend on it, or in this case my family's lives depend on it. I just saw a lot of questions."

Gale looked at her son for a moment. "Take care of your horse and come on in. I kept your supper warm for you."

"Yes'm."

Gale watched him head for the barn, knowing the die was cast. She went back inside and set supper out for him. She sat at the table and began mending the knees of Brenden's pants, a seemingly endless chore. He and the girls were already in bed.

Sean came in and sat down at the table. "Boy, the ham smells awfully good, Ma." He cut into the meat and forked a piece into his mouth. His head nodded with approval. "Tastes good too," he said after he swallowed.

"Thank you, son." Then almost absent mindedly she said, "From now on, when you ride out to the range I think it's best you wear your gun belt."

Sean stopped chewing for a moment and looked at his mother but didn't say anything.

"Did you hear me, son?"

"I did, Ma, it's just you surprised me. Whenever I ask Pa about when I could wear my gun he always says, 'Your mother will know'."

"Your father said that?"

"Yes'm."

"That rascal. He knows me too well."

They both laughed, then Gale became serious. "Well, I think you're ready now. Son, I know firearms are necessary in this country. I trust you'll follow your father's words about their use."

"Pa has taught me well, Ma. I won't misuse them."

Gale took a deep breath and nodded. She folded Brenden's pants and stood. "I'm turning in. Good night, son. I love you."

"I love you too, Ma."

Chapter Eight

JASPER AND BLACK FEATHER RODE into the clan village. The people came out and gathered around them while they put their horses in the corral and unsaddled them. The village sat on the shore of a lake the clan called Sky Water because it was almost always the color of the sky, no matter what the weather. Twenty-one family lodges dotted the area between the lake and the trees. Behind the lodges several women looked up from tending neat rows of maize, potatoes, onion and watermelon. The warm scent of rosemary and thyme filled the air.

"As the sisters told us, Indian Jack is dead," Black Feather announced. "Fire Hawk buried him according to our custom."

Murmurs rippled through the group and Jasper noticed faces showing sadness and appreciation.

A woman came forward. She was thin, her face lined with a long life. Her long white hair fell down her back. Jasper bent down and she put her arms around his neck, pressing her cheek against his.

"Hello, Rain Water."

"My Son, it is good to see you."

"And very good to see you, my Mother."

"Come to our lodge so I can feed you. You look too skinny. Does your white wife not give you enough to eat?"

"Now, Mother, you know she's a good woman."

"Maybe, but she is not a clan woman. You could have done better."

"I'll tell her you said so."

A slight smile curved Rain Water's lips. "I think you keep this to yourself. I am old and cannot fight her fire."

As they walked through the village others came and greeted Jasper. Men grasped his forearm with respect and women touched or hugged him. When they reached the lodge he stooped to enter and took his place as the second son.

Rain Water was the widow of the former chief and Black Feather was next in line to be chief of the clan, after Walks With Bears. The lodge she shared with her son and his family was large. Black Feather had two sisters and they came with their families, so it was a gathering of many, including Black Feather's wife and their two sons.

They all sat in a large circle passing around a meal of venison, rabbit, black beans and maize bread, all seasoned with natural herbs. This was Jasper's kind of meal. He wished he could eat more, but out of respect he politely ate a much smaller portion than he normally did.

Jasper loved his Indian family and the life they had so willingly taught him. A light hearted mood prevailed because of his return but a tinge of sadness colored the conversation. Jasper considered how the clan openly discussed the connection of all living things to one another, while it was rarely a thought in the daily life of so called civilized folks. The loss of one member was a loss to the heart of the whole tribe. Jasper missed that connection in his other world.

When the meal was finished Black Feather motioned for Jasper to follow and led him to another lodge.

"The men who killed Jack and Soft Rain are in there. Talk to them and hear their story so you can tell it when you return to your other home."

Jasper nodded and entered the lodge.

"Well, lookee here," one of the men sneered. "If it ain't the injun lover hisself."

Jasper let his eyes get used to the low light of the single torch and looked at each of the three men. They lay naked, their hands and feet bound with buckskin straps.

"You goin' to shoot us, Jasper Lee?" Jasper recognized Eldon Samson, a known bad man.

"I can pretty much guarantee you'll come to wish I had."

"Go to hell, Lee."

"What's goin' to happen to us?" A younger man asked. Even in the dim light Jasper could see the fear in his eyes.

"It's not up to me. The clan elders will decide whether or not you wronged the clan and if so, the women you violated will tell the elders what they want as punishment."

"Are they goin' to kill us?"

"That ain't what you need to worry about. What you need to worry about is how long it will take you to die."

The young man swallowed hard. "Mr. Lee..."

"Shut up, kid!" Samson yelled.

Jasper stepped over to Samson and yanked his head back with a fistful of hair. "Shut your mouth or I'll cut your tongue out right here."

Samson glared at Jasper.

Jasper let go and Samson's head thumped against the lodge floor. "Go ahead kid. What do you have to say?"

"My folks live in Kentville. Frank and Mary Albright are their names. Could you get a message to them that I'm sorry I brought them so much hurt and embarrassment?" Tears welled in the young man's eyes. "They're good folks and don't deserve what I've done to them."

"What's your name?"

"Larry...well, Lawrence."

"All right, Lawrence. I'll find your folks."

"What about you?" Jasper asked the last man.

"My name's Jess Gestas. I done what I done and that's that."

"Suit yourself."

"Ain't you goin' to ask me, Lee?" Samson asked mockingly.

"I know who and what you are. Do you feel like a man for raping and murdering a helpless young girl? For killin' my kin?"

"Those fools were your kin?"

"My Pa and my brothers."

"Ya don't say! Yeah, it felt good when I put that bullet hole in your old man's head and your brother's face."

Jasper's teeth clenched as his hand touched the grip of this right pistol.

"C'mon Jasper, you know you wanna kill me."

Jasper's hand dropped from his gun and he knelt down close to Samson's face. "Before too long, Samson, you're goin' to be beggin' me to shoot you."

Samson spit in Jasper's face but Jasper didn't miss the fear in the man's eyes.

Jasper wiped off the spit and looked at Samson's leg. "It looks like someone sliced you up a bit."

"One of your brothers did that to him, Mr. Lee."

"Shut your goddamn mouth, kid!"

"That would've been Caleb." Jasper's fingers rubbed against his holster and he had to force himself not to draw. "He always was feisty."

"Yeah, well he died just like the rest of your family, Lee."

Jasper walked to the lodge opening and half turned. "They died quicker than you will, Samson."

Deep concern weighed heavy on Dr. Amos Scoville. Nancy Norton didn't show up for her appointment which was not like her. Newly pregnant with her first child, she was very conscientious about following the doctor's advice. The doctor had asked old Tom Rogers, a retired peace officer, to ride out to the Norton place and check on things. Tom returned...alone.

Amos stepped out to his porch. "What'd you find out, Tom?"

"Something ain't right, Doc. The place is closed up and there's a notice on the door sayin' that scoundrel Cornell Norris bought the Norton's out and they went back east."

"That's preposterous! The Nortons would never sell. That ranch was their life!"

"Easy, Doc, you're preachin' to the choir."

Amos deflated, tears rimming his eyes. "Tom, please come inside. I have a great favor to ask of you."

Amos sat down at his desk, wrote a message, sealed it in an envelope, and handed it to Tom.

"You know whatever goes through the telegraph here is reported to Norris and his cronies."

"That's a fact."

"I'm asking you to ride to Lowell Town and send this message by telegraph there. I fear the Nortons have been murdered. The law can't be trusted here and something needs to be done."

"But who can you trust to do something about it?"

"My former commanding officer when I was a regimental surgeon."

"Who's that?"

"Ulysses S. Grant."

"Jumpin' Jehoshaphat, Doc! I didn't know you know'd the president!"

"Well I do, Tom."

Tom took the envelope. "This ol' broken down peace officer can't move very fast, but my horse, Shooter, can. We'll ride like the wind."

"Thank you, Tom."

Chapter Nine

THE PEOPLE WERE GATHERED AROUND the elders in the glow of fires and torches.

The chief listed the things the white men had done and a murmur rumbled through the gathering. He called for Moon on the Water to step forward to say what she wanted done to them.

The young woman struggled to stand, obviously in pain. "My father is dead. My sister is dead." She pointed to her other sister. "We are ruined, so no warrior will have us."

Jasper noticed Claw of the Eagle bow his head at Moon on the Water's statement. When his face rose, tears glistened in the firelight.

"The white men killed Soft Rain by filling her with big sticks where they wanted her womanhood because she fought them and hurt them. They pushed the sticks hard into her, tearing her inside. She died when her blood ran out.

"My sister, Butterfly Wing, and I want these men to die slowly. Before they die we want to push sticks into them so they can feel the pain of Soft Rain. Then we will cut off their manhood."

Jasper felt himself involuntarily clenching his jaws and squeezing the muscles at the bottom of his groin at Moon on the Water's descriptions. He had no doubt Moon on the Water could do the deeds she described, but Butterfly Wing sat with her head down and said nothing.

The chief motioned for Moon on the Water to sit again. The elders conferred for a short while. Then the chief stood.

"The punishment for the white men shall be the Circle of Fire. Before the men die the sisters may have their revenge on them."

Some warriors went to the lodge while others began to sink three large poles in the ground. The naked white men were put in front of the people, still trussed in buckskin. The firelight played over the men's bodies as they struggled to hold their knees together to hide their genitals. Some people threw small stones at the men, then more started throwing until soon the entire village was throwing the small stones.

The white men were not seriously injured by the stones but they cowered and yelped like children being spanked. Their clumsy dance raised a dust cloud that caught the firelight and created a glowing red circle around them. Gestas fell to the ground and the people laughed as the men's faces flushed with humiliation.

"Stop it you goddamn sons of bitches!" Samson screamed. He tried to lunge at a young boy but a warrior knocked him back.

"C'mon you son of a bitch! Untie me and fight me like a man!"

The warrior grabbed Samson by the hair and pulled him so that their faces were inches apart. "You are not worthy of the honor to fight a warrior. You only fight old men and women. You are nothing!" The warrior growled. He threw Samson into the dirt.

Three cries from the warriors who sank the poles brought the stoning to a halt. They grabbed the men and dragged them to the three silent sentries. Samson and Gestas yelled and screamed, the only thing they could do in the way of a struggle. Lawrence didn't offer any resistance.

The men faced each other around a pile of cut wood and branches, each had their hands tied behind their pole. Each pole stood five paces from the pile of wood. Their feet were spread wide and staked. When it came time to tie Samson's feet, he kicked a warrior in the face. The warrior kneed Samson in the groin and punched him in the head. Samson hung on his pole muttering curse words.

Satisfied the men were securely tied, the warriors brought the sisters to the pile of wood. Each sister carried a small torch which they placed inside the bottom the pile. Soon smoke spiraled into the night, set aglow by flames taking up the chase of the ghostly wisps.

The fire didn't begin large but after the pile started to burn down the chief nodded to a person who walked to the fire and put on more wood. When that wood burned brightly the chief nodded to the next person and so on. Through this process the fire gradually grew in size. The chief nodded to Jasper. Jasper was hesitant but he rose and walked to the fire. Now fully recognizing what the punishment would be, his denial evaporated. He struggled inside. To him justice should be swift and sure, not a drawn out torture. He briefly toyed with the idea of shooting the men but dismissed the thought. These men wronged the clan in the clan's territory. The right to justice belonged to them and only them.

He looked at Samson. Red eyes glared through the shadows dancing across his face, creating a demon's mask.

"Hey, Lee, you're just as stupid as these redskins. All you're doing is keeping us nice and warm."

Jasper placed his wood on the fire without a reply. In time, the fire would speak for him.

Hours passed as the process continued. The three men began to yell for water and twisted and turned their bodies in vain to avoid the heat. The ropes rubbed their skin raw and eventually cut bleeding wounds. On Jasper's fourth turn his stomach turned at the odor beginning to build. All three men were gasping and struggling for breath, their skin bright red.

"Water! For God's sake man, bring us water!" Gestas begged.

The young one, Lawrence, was hanging limp and moaning.

Samson's head hung low, but he raised it to look at Jasper. Those red eyes glowed with hatred. "Go fuck yourself, you son of a bitch, you're lettin' them cook us to death!" Then Samson screamed as the skin on his stomach started to split, his intestines bulging through. Soon the intestines began to sizzle. Samson screamed until his screams became exhausted whimpers.

Jasper turned and walked back to his seat still carrying his wood.

The Chief nodded to Moon On The Water and she struggled to her feet. Claw Of The Eagle jumped up to help her. They looked into each other's eyes for a moment, then she turned to Butterfly Wing but she slowly shook her head.

Moon On The Water straightened her back and walked to the fire. Claw Of The Eagle followed her, carrying three lengths of blackberry branches with a cloth at one end to protect his hands from the thorns. She stopped in front of Gestas. The man's eyes glared at her but he couldn't speak. Moon On The Water took a blackberry branch from Claw Of The Eagle and grasped it on the end with the cloth. Bending down in front of the man, she put the branch against his anus and shoved as hard as she could.

The sound the man made wasn't a scream. It was the most primal testament to pain Jasper had ever heard come from a living creature. Then the man made another guttural sound as Moon On The Water sliced off his penis, held it up and then threw it into the fire.

Jasper's whole body tensed tightly as he forced the contents of this stomach to stay down. He thought Soft Rain may have made the same sounds.

Moon On The Water walked over to Lawrence, grabbed his hair and pulled his face up so she could look at him. Jasper rose and started to them. He heard Lawrence speak to her.

"I'm s-s-sorry for what I- I've done. D-d-do what you need to, b-b- but I just ask y-you to f-forgive me."

Moon On The Water cocked her head to the side and looked at the dying man. She leaned forward, putting her moving lips close to his ear as she slipped her blade under his ribs and drove it into his heart. He gurgled for a few moments and then was gone. Moon On The Water then inserted the blade in the bottom of Lawrence's bulging stomach, slicing up, causing gas and bloody fluid to spurt and bubble out, filling the air with a putrid odor. Lawrence's body seemed to shrink and collapse into itself, a sight that seared into Jasper's mind. The thought of Lawrence's parents made him lower and shake his head.

Moon On The Water moved to Samson. His intestines were now bulging more and she couldn't bend down in front of him.

"Go to hell, bitch," he growled hoarsely.

He started to say something else, but as his mouth opened Moon On The Water shoved a blackberry branch into his throat. He struggled and gagged. She bent down, sliced off his penis and held it in front of him. His eyes were wide and turning glassy. She threw his penis in the flames and walked out of the Circle of Fire. Then she bolted into the night, leaving a stunned and confused Claw Of The Eagle standing at the edge of the village.

Seconds later, Samson's intestines exploded. Not long after, Gestas's stomach also cracked and exploded. People gagged on the ghastly smell of burnt flesh, excrement and stomach acid permeating the air. The Chief gathered his wood and a line formed behind him. Everyone threw their last wood on the blaze. Warriors, using wide buckskin straps, pulled the posts and laid them and the men on the pyre. Spark and smoke carried their remains into the emptiness of the uneasy night.

The people quietly made their way to their lodges. Jasper saw no joy or satisfaction in their faces, only empty bloodshot eyes and grim lines around their mouths. He crawled into his bed roll, his stomach roiling, his body and emotions drained, leaving only an empty, hollow feeling.

Chapter Ten

THOUGH EXHAUSTED, sleep did not find Jasper. He lay in his bedroll trying to sort his emotions until the glow of the new day began to filter through the flap of the lodge. He rose silently, walking out to face the rising sun. Dropping to one knee he offered his morning prayer to Father Sun but it did not bring the peace that usually came when he started a new day with his clan family.

"My son has dark thoughts about last night?" The whisper he had hoped for came and he looked to see Rain Water standing beside him.

He nodded and she sat down beside him.

"I would think less of you if you didn't. It is true the punishment was very harsh, but there is a reason."

"I can't find a reason in my mind."

"Of course not. Although you are a member of the clan you are a white man and live the white man way. You really cannot feel the fear we have. Most white men do not care for the Creator's earth or the creatures of Father Sun and Sister Wind as we do. They are many and have stronger weapons than we do. We know we must put fear in them to keep the bad of the white man away.

"Would you have punished a clan member the same way if he did the same thing?"

Mother smiled, but her eyes were amber pools of sadness. "Before you knew us; before the white man came, we had no warriors. When I was a young girl we did not have to fight. We lived in peace, hunted and fished. We gathered roots, nuts, berries and fruits to live. We welcomed all who came to our village, shared what we could and traded our baskets, robes and other things we made. It was a happy life.

"Then the white man came. The first ones seemed to like us. They only took what they needed from the land and the water. They treated us like brothers and sisters. But more came. They began to take our land and kill the animals we needed to survive so they could sell the fur to others. When we told them to stop they spoke to us with dirty tongues. But we are not stupid. We saw through them and decided to fight for what the spirits had given us.

"We learned we must frighten those white men or they would make us disappear from this world. We fought hard enough to make the white chiefs want to make a treaty. The treaty took land from us but gave us land we no longer must fight for.

"Because we are a peaceful people by nature, we do not have men who would harm clan members. We do not have to punish any clan member that way. But, because we are becoming more like the white man, I fear this will change."

"Mother, I'm sorry. I didn't mean to say the punishment wasn't true. I'm a member of this clan. Your fears are my fears for I love you all. The white man word 'justice' even means different things to different white men. Many believe the natural law, which I learned from Pa...and from you, is too harsh."

"As a clan member it is your task to tell the white men what happened to those who wronged us. Make them understand we are not powerless. In our own way we understand your word 'justice.' Justice was done last night."

He looked into Rain Water's eyes. "I feel the spirits are taking me on a journey. I don't know why but my task is to learn what true justice means."

Rain Water put her hand on Jasper's forehead as tears formed in her eyes. "My son, I have waited many winters for you to hear the spirits. You have a good heart with a strong and true spirit. You must find your spirit guide and ask him to help you find your way."

Jasper rose and helped Rain Water to her feet. "Thank you, Mother. You've always been the center of my circle. You've always kept me from wandering too far."

"You are always in my heart, Fire Hawk." She put her hands on his cheeks. "Find the star and keep it close to your heart."

"What star? I don't understand."

"With the help of kindred spirits, you will."

The rising sun speared new shafts of light through the trees when Jasper and Rain Water arrived at the meeting circle. Moon On The Water stood in the middle. She held her head high but her eyes were red as they looked out in the distance. Her hair was matted on one side and Jasper could tell she had slept out in the woods. Butterfly Wing sat with her head down, tears falling from her eyes.

Black Feather came and stood next to Jasper on one side, Rain Water on the other.

She touched his arm. "I know what you want to say. Ask Walks With Bears if you can speak.

Jasper cleared his throat. "Walks With Bears, my Chief, I would like to speak to the clan."

The chief looked around. "We will all listen to Fire Hawk's words."

Jasper stood next to the sisters. "My clan, my family. I know the way of the people is to banish women who have been ruined."

Butterfly Wing sobbed.

"I have told Black Feather that I'll take the sisters to work on my ranches until they're ready to decide their future. But I'm not sure that's the true answer here. I ask you all to think about another way. I want to ask this gathering if there are any men who would want to join with the sisters. I think it is a question that should be asked before banishment. I ask Chief Walks With Bears to consider asking this question."

The chief looked at Jasper with a steady gaze for a long moment. Then he looked around at the gathered clan.

"Are there men in this clan who would join with either of the sisters?"

For a few seconds no one moved. Then Claw Of The Eagle slowly rose to his feet.

Moon On The Water still looked straight ahead, but she trembled.

Claw Of The Eagle walked toward her with a slow but deliberate stride until he intercepted her stare. Then their eyes met and with a sob Moon On The Water rushed to Claw Of The Eagle, wrapping her arms around his neck. He held her close and whispered in her ear. Her body shook as she openly cried.

All eyes were now on Butterfly Wing who hadn't moved a muscle. A slight commotion arose from the rear of the gathering. The warrior, Wind Runner, pushed his way forward. Jasper's breath caught. Wind Runner was the largest and fiercest warrior in the clan and never known to be gentle with anything or anybody. He had the demeanor of a fighter and a face that seemed perpetually set for battle. Jasper was about to stop Wind Runner, but Mother's eyes told him not to interfere.

Wind Runner knelt in front of Butterfly Wing who still sat with her legs tucked to her side. He put his hand under her chin bringing her face up to his.

"Do you fear me, Butterfly Wing?"

She moved her head side to side.

"They say I am a great warrior but I am not good at talking to women." He took a deep breath. "I have loved you since we were children but I did not know how to tell you and I was afraid you would reject me, as I am now." He took another deep breath. "I wish us to join. I will love you, protect you and help you heal. I offer you my lodge and my life, if you will have me."

Jasper thought Butterfly Wing might be in shock because she simply looked into Wind Runner's eyes for a long time. Then she leaned forward, brushing her lips against his forehead, his cheeks and his lips. She rubbed his nose with hers before collapsing into his chest.

Wind Runner gently picked her up and held her like she was a feather, for once battle gone from his face.

A feeling of surprise and great relief flowed through the clan. Sounds of happy approval began to build. Walks With Bears raised his hands in a command for quiet. He stepped in front of the two couples with the smile befitting a happy father.

"I expected this and asked the spirits for guidance. They approve of this joining. You have showed us a new and better way, Fire Hawk. When Father Sun rises again we will prepare a celebration."

The clan gathered around the couples with smiles, offering congratulations.

Jasper turned and started for the corral to get Coal, but Rain Water pulled on his arm.

"Thank you, my son. You helped us accept a new and better way."

"I could see in everyone's heart they didn't want the sisters to leave. I just didn't want the sisters to suffer more when they did nothing wrong. I guess it's just another way of seeing justice is done."

Rain Water gazed steadily into Jasper's eyes for a moment and then smiled. "You must stay for the celebration."

"I wish I could but I still have men to find."

"Take Black Feather with you and maybe Wind Runner."

"Black Feather will know if I need him...and Wind Runner needs to be with his woman now."

Rain Water brought his face down with her gentle hands and brushed her lips on his cheek. "Listen to the spirits and remember my words, Fire Hawk... and come back."

"I never forget your words, Mother, and I will come back. Please don't worry."

But Jasper saw the worry in Rain Water's eyes before he turned and headed for the corral.

Chapter Eleven

JUDGE RANCE IVERSON SIPPED his Kentucky bourbon while he listened to the governor.

"As you know, Rance, my sister means the world to me. It's not her fault her no account husband gave her a bad seed. She would just die if he swung."

"Murder and rape are serious crimes, Governor."

"Yes, yes, I know, but not so bad when it's an old sodbuster and his ignorant sons. And the girl, well, probably just a country floozy."

"It would put me in a tough position."

"I understand, but you're a tough man. That's why I'm recommending you to replace me when I become a United States Senator after we become a state."

"I'll give this matter some thought. I'm concerned about this cowboy, Rich Delton, though. According to the report I've seen, he's an eyewitness to the crimes you're nephew committed."

"Allegedly committed." The governor shot back. "But I hear the good folks of Lowell Town are mighty upset at that Delton boy. There's a lot of talk about a lynchin'."

"That's not likely to happen as long as Stan Barstow is the town marshal. He's a tough, honest lawman."

The governor leaned forward in his chair. "Rance, Delton won't make it to court."

Iverson's swallow of bourbon went down hard.

"Now, this Jasper Lee fellow is a problem. I'm quite sure he's the only person who cares one wit about what happened in Arlington. What I need you to do is issue an arrest warrant for Jasper Lee on thirteen counts of murder in the first degree. That should distract folks about Bart."

"I'll need the prosecutor to send me the charges."

"He will."

Iverson gave the governor a quizzical look.

"Who do think is going to replace you as judge?"

Charlie Forbes eyed the rider trotting towards the ranch office and rested his hand on his pistol. Several cowboys had come by looking for work in the last couple of weeks, but he sent them on after giving them a meal. He'd have to do the same with this man.

"You the foreman?"

"I am..."

"Name's John Smith. The governor said you'd have a job for me," the man said before Charlie could tell him the score.

"The governor, eh. You done any cow punchin'?"

"Oh yeah, plenty."

Charlie looked at the horse this John Smith rode in to the ranch. "I don't see any chaps or rope on that horse."

"Look, the governor said you'd have a job for me. I don't think you wanna piss him off."

Charlie gave Smith a hard look. "You'll have a job...right up to the time you talk to me like that again. You understand?"

"Okay, okay, I understand."

"Put your horse away and get some vittles over at the bunkhouse. We start work at sun up. Be ready."

"I will."

Charlie went back into his office and continued going over the brand count. Thirty minutes later a commotion outside interrupted his count. He stepped out to find Smith sitting in the dirt in front of the bunkhouse door. Three other young cowboys surrounded him, one holding a pistol by the top of the cylinder.

"What the hell's going on here?"

"He's what's going on," Jerry Sanchez nodded to Smith.

"You got a problem with Smith?"

"Smith? This here's Bart Moore, a lyin', back-stabbin' low life."

"Moore, eh." Charlie rubbed his hand over his chin then across the back of his neck. You kin to the governor's sister?"

"I'm the governor's nephew! You'd better watch out what you do."

"You bringin' him on, Charlie? Because if you do, I'm quittin'."

"That'll make three of us," Walt Winters added and his brother nodded in agreement.

Charlie walked over, picked up Moore's hat and lifted him up by the arm. He plopped the hat on Moore's head sending a cloud of dust flying around the outlaw. "Is that his pistol?"

"Yeah, we took it from him after he pulled it on us."

Charlie took the pistol, emptied it and gave it to Moore. "Get your horse and get out. Tell the governor he can't afford you workin' here."

Moore glared. "You're going to regret this."

Forbes laughed. "Not likely." His eyes narrowed. "Now, get out."

Jasper rode Coal at an easy lope for a good four hours, occasionally stopping to check his back trail. Although his eyes constantly scanned his surroundings, his thoughts kept going over the night before. He tried to sort out what he witnessed, indeed what he took part in, and his own idea of what constituted fair justice. Jasper knew many people believed his past levies of justice were harsh…even cruel, because he acted swiftly and finally. He rarely took time to hear a man's story. His thoughts continued without resolution.

He rode up the Seneca River and eased Coal into a thicket of trees. He scanned the area for anything out of place. The river was running fairly strong, its azure waters undulating like a giant serpent. The day had become warm and annoying insects darted around Jasper, but he remained still.

He narrowed his eyes at a shadow behind some tall brush across the river. It appeared to be a horse. Then he saw a man sitting against a tree on the opposite bank near the river's edge. Jasper pulled out his telescope. The man had a large blotch of blood around his right shoulder. Jasper recognized the man as Harry Wells, an off and on outlaw that had ridden in his regiment during the war. A scan of the area didn't turn up anything else.

Jasper urged Coal out of the trees and eased him into the water. Near the middle of the river the cold water came up over Jasper's high top moccasins. It felt good against the heat of the day. When they got to the other side Coal climbed the bank and Jasper dismounted. He let Coal stay to drink and walked over to Wells.

Harry's eyes were closed and Jasper noticed his breathing was labored.

"Harry? It's Jasper Lee."

Harry's eyelids fluttered open. "Well howdy, Jasper. Long time no see."

"Looks like you lost an argument."

"Son-of-a-bitch shot me in the back."

"Who?"

"Dewey Cann, I think."

"He rides with Bart Moore, don't he?"

"Yeah, so did I."

Jasper gave Harry a hard stare.

"C'mon, Jasper. You've knowed me long enough to know I might get a little squirrelly sometimes, but I ain't never killed men in cold blood and I sure as hell ain't forced myself on no women."

"Were you the rider that met the gang at Arlington and Tully Valley Road?"

Harry nodded. "Yeah, I got a belly full of whiskey a couple of nights before the boys left Kentville and shot up a saloon. They threw me in the jail for five days. I went lookin' for the boys after that."

"You know what they did."

"Yeah, that crazy idiot Bart Moore and some of the others bragged all about it."

"Why did you stay with 'em."

"Well, Jasper, I was going to leave 'em but it appears you were the one who shot us all up in Tully Valley. I didn't know what the hell was goin' on until Moore told us you were the one. I knew I had nothin' to fear from you because I didn't do what they did so I decided to get out of the territory. That's when Cann shot me."

"Let me look at that wound." Jasper unbuttoned Harry's shirt and carefully inspected the injury. "If I can get you to a healer soon enough you might make it. Can you ride?"

"I don't know, Jasper." Harry took a deep breath and looked around him. "I was kinda thinkin' dyin' might not be so bad since I ain't amounted to much my whole life and this place looked as good as any for my bones to rest."

Jasper put his hand on Harry's other shoulder. "Harry, you've done good things in your life, along with the bad. I know you were a good soldier. Maybe this is what you needed to change yourself around."

"Well, the closest town is Kentville. I wouldn't last ten seconds there."

"I'm not takin' you to Kentville. I'll make a poultice for that wound, then I'll take you to the clan. They're family to me and they'll take care of you."

"I'm not sure I can stay awake for the ride."

"Don't worry, I'll truss you up good and tight."

Jasper guided Harry's horse for two hours before he noticed the ropes were beginning to loosen. He dismounted and started working on tightening them. A hawk called out and Jasper looked up to see it circling above. He caught the red tinge along the edge of the hawk's tail feathers...a red-tailed hawk, his clan namesake. He nodded to the bird and continued tightening the ropes on Harry.

Suddenly wings flapped behind him. He turned to see the hawk sitting on his saddle, gazing at him.

Surprised for a moment, Jasper finally found his tongue. "Afternoon, Hawk."

The hawk's gaze was fixed and Jasper found himself gazing back and getting drawn into those dark eyes. He felt, rather than heard a voice.

"I am your spirit guide, but you are a hard one to give counsel to because you do not take the time to listen."

"I'm sorry, Hawk, I meant no disrespect."

"I felt no disrespect, but listen now. Follow the trail but know there are strong forces working against you. Be alert and cautious. Do not judge every one by how they look. The outwardly meek often have great strength and courage in their hearts. Trust those with clear eyes and clean tongue. Trust those who love you."

"Sound words, Hawk. I will keep them in my heart."

With a flap of great wings, Hawk took to the air.

Jasper stood silently for awhile trying to understand what just happened. Harry's moan brought Jasper back to the task at hand.

When Jasper arrived at the clan, Rain Water immediately ordered Harry to be brought to the family lodge. Rain Water, a holy woman and a healer, immediately went to work with the help of Black Feather's wife.

Jasper walked out of the lodge with Black Feather feeling better now that Harry was in good hands.

"Now you must stay for the celebration, Fire Hawk. Father Sun is going for his rest and soon we will light the fires."

"I'll stay, my Brother, but I'll leave before Father Sun rises again."

Black Feather put a hand on Jasper's shoulder and smiled.

The sunset set the clouds aglow casting a light show across the blue sky. Claw Of The Eagle and Moon On The Water stood facing Wind Runner and Butterfly Wing.

Each couple wore matching headbands made of the white and black eagle feathers and multi-colored beads. Moon On The Water's proud face glowed in the sun's rays. Butterfly Wing's mouth bore a slight smile as she leaned against Wind Runner, who held her with a protective arm. The women didn't seem to mind they had no time to make their joining dresses. They both wore necklaces and ankle bracelets made by other women in the clan.

The chief stepped between the two couples and cleared his throat. "I, Walks With Bears, say it is time for the joining."

A young girl came forward and handed the chief a decorated

leather tie.

He turned to Claw Of The Eagle and Moon On The Water. "We offer this tie and with it the blessings of Father Sun, Mother Earth and the Clan Of The Hawk. By this tying may you be forever joined in life."

He performed the same ritual with Wind Runner and Butterfly Wing then stepped back into the circle. "May your joining be filled with happiness and bring forth children who will make our clan strong and bring harmony for all."

Still joined by the ties, the couples walked through the happy people heading for their lodges. They stopped in front of Jasper. The sisters each touched his hands and nodded to him. He nodded back. The people sang and danced well into the night, celebrating the new families and the new way.

The sun had not yet shown when Jasper tied his bedroll and quietly started for the lodge door.

"Jasper," Harry whispered.

Jasper bent down near him. "Feelin' better, Harry?"

"A might. I wanted to thank you for bringin' me here and getting me fixed up."

"I'm glad I found you."

"Listen, Jasper. Bart Moore was braggin' that his uncle was goin' to take care of their problems, including you. You gotta be careful."

"I will. Where's the gang?"

"A day's ride north of Kentville, where the Seneca and Muddy creek meet. They stay in and around an old cabin."

"Yeah, I know the area. Thanks, Harry, and you rest up."

"Good luck, Jasper. I think you'll need it."

Chapter Twelve

BART MOORE RODE INTO THE CAMP where the other men waited and jumped off his horse.

"What are you doin' back here so soon?" Dewey Cann asked.

Moore stomped over to the campfire and kicked dirt into a choking cloud. Then he grabbed the coffee pot and smashed it against a tree. "I'm back because my uncle lets assholes run his ranch!"

"What did they do?"

"What did they do?! They kicked me off the place, that's what they did! Me! Bart Moore!"

Nobody said anything. Moore stood there with an ugly twist to his mouth, his face flushed and his fists tightly clenched.

"What do you want us to do, Bart?"

"I've been thinking about that." Moore looked at the four remaining members of his gang. "Where's Harry?"

"He lit a shuck, but he ain't going far."

"Whaddya mean?"

"He said he was leavin' the territory, got on his horse and started riding off. He said some bad things about you and your uncle, so I plugged him in the back."

"You drop him?"

"No, he still rode off, but he ain't goin' far."

Moore looked at his men for a minute, gauging them against a hatching plan. "All right, gettin' back to my plans. I don't know about you guys but I'm tired of living this bullshit life. We do little stuff here and there and we got nothin' to show for it. It's time we hit it big so we can enjoy a little of the good life."

"Sounds good to us, Bart," Cann said. "What big hit do you have in mind?"

"How does robbin' the Kentville Bank sound?"

"Now you're talkin'. There's big money there for sure."

"Yeah there is, but we'll have to be careful because of the guards. I've been in the area where the vault is with my uncle. I know how we can do this but everyone has to follow the plan."

"We're with ya, Bart."

Chapter Thirteen

STAN BARSTOW SAT IN THE FOYER of the office of the federal judge for the territory. The door to the judge's office opened and a man motioned for him to enter. The man Stan thought to be the judge rose from a chair behind a large desk.

"Marshal Barstow, welcome."

"Thank you, sir."

"I'm Judge Abramson."

"Nice to meet you, Judge."

"The gentleman standing next to you is Mr. Robert Rawley."

"Nice to meet you, Mr. Rawley."

"Same here, Marshal."

Please sit, gentlemen," the judge said. "How was your trip, Marshal?"

"Pleasurable, sir, on a day like this."

Both other men nodded in agreement.

The judge leaned forward. "Marshal, I asked you to come for a very important reason. I'm sure you're aware of the corruption in the government of the territory and the crime that is going on here."

"I hear things from time to time about the corruption. I'm well aware of the crime problem."

"Well, it's been of much concern to me and to Washington. The president received a message from a friend in Kentville who alleges serious crimes on the part of the governor. The United States Attorney General asked me for a recommendation for a man the president could appoint as the US Marshal for the territory. I sent him your name."

Stan sat stunned for a moment. "Well, I'm honored, sir, but there's already a US Marshal for the territory."

"Yes, there is and he is a good man also, but he's decided to resign and move to Oregon."

"Okay, why me?"

"You have a reputation of being a fair and tough lawman. I've read some of your reports and I'm impressed with your investigative skills. I believe you're the man for the job. Mr. Rawley is a Deputy Attorney General. He came here to fill you in on your responsibilities and what's expected of you, if you decide to accept the appointment."

Stan turned to Rawley. "I'm interested, but I'd like to hear what you have to say before I make up my mind."

"Smart man. If you decide to take the job, in addition to the normal duties of a US Marshal, we want you investigate and bring down the governor and his cronies."

"That's a pretty tall order."

"We know. We'll create a special fund to make sure you have the resources necessary to do the job. You'll be able to hire deputies and pay them a higher rate than deputy marshal's currently make as long as they're focused on this matter. We also have resources through the judge here to help you with obtaining any documentation you may need. In other words, we'll support you any way we can."

"I really don't want to stop being the Lowell Town Marshal."

"You can keep your position as the Lowell Town Marshal, if you like, as long as it doesn't interfere with your primary mission."

Stan rose from his seat and walked to a window and studied the outside for a minute, then turned and faced the two officials. "This kind of investigation could put my family in danger."

Rawley put his hand to his chin. "Hmm, we didn't think about that." He was quiet for a few minutes as he thought through the question. "I'll take care of it. If there's danger to your family bring them here to Ft. Hurley. We'll put them under federal protection and the Army will take care of them until I can make arrangements to temporarily move them out of the territory."

"How much does the job pay?"

"Ninety dollars a month," Rawley answered.

Stan looked down at his hands for a moment. "All right, I'll accept the appointment."

Rawley looked relieved. "Good. The president already took the liberty to submit your name to Congress and they approved your appointment."

The judge came from behind his desk with a bible. "Marshal, please stand and raise your right hand."

Black Feather rode toward the Lee ranch house. "Hello, the ranch!"

Sean came out with his Winchester, but when he saw Black Feather he set it inside. "Uncle, it's good to see you!"

Black Feather eased his horse forward and dismounted. The two embraced. "It is good to see you too, Sean."

Gale came out of the house. Concern etched deep lines across her forehead.

"Hello, sister." Black Feather came up on the porch and gave her a hug. "Jasper is well. I brought you a letter."

Gale took the letter and returned Black Feather's hug. "Please come in and have some coffee."

"That sounds good."

After the family was settled around the table, Black Feather related the events since Jasper left to bring justice to those who murdered his pa, brothers and Claire Dolan.

"His task is nearly done. He believes there are only five men left, including the leader, Bart Moore."

"Has he killed all of them?"

"No, not all. Some will be judged by white man's justice. We judged others."

Gale chose not to inquire further into Black Feather's statement.

A slight smile crossed Black Feather's face. "Jasper told me all that has happened. He will find the others and do what is right according to natural law."

Gale put her hand on Black Feather's, tears welling in her eyes. "You're a good brother and know my husband well."

Black Feather rose. "Thank you for the coffee. I must get back to the clan and be ready if Fire Haw...uh, Jasper needs me."

"It's all right to use his clan name here, Black Feather," Gale said. "We're proud of it."

Black Feather stood silent for a moment. "Sister, it is nearing time for Sean to go on his first vision quest."

Sean stood up. "I'm ready, Uncle!"

Gale looked at her oldest son. "We know you're ready, Sean, but you'll have to wait 'til your father comes back so the work will get done."

"I know, Ma, but you'll let me go then?"

"Yes, Sean."

The boy's face broke out in a large grin.

Black Feather put his hand on Gale's shoulder. "It is also time for you, sister."

She put her hand on his. "Thank you, brother, but I'm not sure Rain Water would approve."

"She has told me many times she asks the spirits to bring you to us. She would be your guide on your quest."

"Rain Water would be my guide?"

"She is a holy woman and a healer. She knows your fire and your love for Fire Hawk. She would be honored to be your guide."

Gale took a deep breath. "I'll consider it, brother. I'll consider it."

Black Feather patted her shoulder, nodded to the children and left.

The kerosene lamp flickered across the paper that Gale unfolded. The children's soft breathing drifted out from their bedrooms. The rooms Jasper had just finished expanding a few weeks ago. She yearned for him, but the scrap of paper connected her to him for now, so Gale read:

My Love,

As I write this letter a full moon is glowing, our moon. I miss you so terribly and I want this action to be over, but these men must be brought to justice. If I do not do it their deeds will be forgotten and such deeds must never be, but I seem to be getting confused over what is the right thing to do with such men. I saw three of them punished in a horrible way and I was revolted by the spectacle. Part of me thought two of them deserved it, but I did not think the other did because he showed remorse. Is that a reason to let a man live after he's participated in brutal murders? I am searching for the answer.

It seems when I am away from you I feel like I am drifting without an anchor. You are my anchor and the center of my life.

I will be home as soon as I possibly can. Kiss the children for me.

Your loving husband,

Jasper

A tear splashed on to the paper. *Oh, how I love that man.* She smiled and she laid her head on her pillow, the letter held against her heart.

Chapter Fourteen

STAN BARSTOW WAS LOST IN THOUGHT about the information Deputy Attorney General Rawley told him concerning the disappearance of the Nortons. He was surprised to see an agitated crowd in front of the Lowell Town Marshal's office. He pushed his horse through the crowd and slid off.

"What's going on?" He worked his way through the door, stopping short as shock, despair and anger slammed into him all at once. Coy Jeffers, his young deputy, lay dead on the floor, shot in the back. He knelt and touched Coy's body. He wanted to roll him over but knew for now he couldn't. His fists clenched and he fought back tears.

"Over here, Marshal," a voice said from one of the jail cells.

Stan slowly stood, walked back and saw Rich Delton's body lying on his cot riddled with bullet holes. "Who did this?" Anger choked at the words.

No one spoke as he looked around, but Bernie Reinholdt looked back at him with knowing eyes.

"Stan, is that a US Marshal's badge you're wearing?" Warren Buck, a town council member asked.

"Yes, it is, Warren. I'm now the US Marshal for the territory."

"Does that mean you can no longer be the town marshal?"

"No it doesn't. I'll explain to the council as soon as you call a meeting, but for now I'll need everyone to clear the office so I can begin an investigation. Can you please get Doc Evanson over here? I'll also need to talk to everyone who is here later."

"You bet, Stan," Buck said and hurried out the door.

The crowd started filing out of the office, but Stan noticed Bernie hanging back.

"Bernie, can you help me for a minute?"

Bernie hesitated, but walked over to the desk.

"I get the feeling you want to tell me something."

"I don't know, Stan. I'm right nervous about this."

"Bernie, if you know something, you need to tell me. They killed Coy, for God's sake."

"Will you keep it confidential?"

"As long as I can, but if there's a trial you might have to testify."

Bernie swallowed hard. "I saw them."

"You saw the men who did this?"

"Yeah, and I've seen both of them before."

"Where?"

"Right here in Lowell Town, the last time the governor came through. The same men are part of the group that ride with the governor when he goes on a campaign stump."

"How did you remember them?"

"One of them gave my daughter Sally a dangerous look and I took notice of this face. He has a long, deep scar on the right side. The other one is a half-breed Mexican."

Stan put his hand on Bernie's shoulder. "Thanks. That's very important information."

Bernie's eyes had the look of a rabbit being chased by a coyote.

"Bernie, I won't tell anyone about this conversation unless we bring these men to trial. If that happens I'll make sure you and your family are protected."

Bernie nodded. "Okay, Stan, I trust you."

"Thanks, Bernie."

Buck brought Doc Evanson through the door of the office.

Doc looked at Coy's body and let out a low, "Oh, my dear God."

"Thanks for coming, Doc. I'm going to need your help with this investigation."

"I'll do whatever I can, Stan. I can't believe they killed Coy. He was such a nice kid."

"He was a good *man*," Stan replied.

Doc simply nodded.

"I'm going to need you to establish the time of death and recover the bullets you can from both bodies."

"Both bodies?!"

"Yeah, they killed my prisoner too."

"Damn. Well then we'd better get to work."

Jasper found the gang's campsite and followed their trail. They were headed for Kentville. He guided Coal through the brush and trees in between the road and the Seneca River, keeping an eye out for any movement. He reined the stallion to a stop when the gang's trail became confused and merged with the tracks of a wagon.

He listened and scanned the area for any movement...nothing. Jasper dismounted and walked Coal to the center of the road. Blood stained the dirt. His eyes traced the tracks of the wagon into a stand of trees on the left side of the road. He carefully followed the tracks until a wagon with no horse attached appeared.

A young man leaned motionless against the back of the seat, his open eyes staring up at the criss cross of branches. Jasper reached over and felt the man's neck then shut the blank eyes. Whimpering from the back of the wagon interrupted Jasper's short prayer. He walked to its side and saw a young woman who had been beaten, her blouse torn open, her skirt bunched around her waist exposing a naked lower torso. Blood stained her thighs.

Jasper retrieved his blanket and bandages from Coal. His jaw tightened as he climbed on to the wagon.

The woman turned her head toward him and screamed.

Jasper raised his open palms and said, "Easy, ma'am. I'm not going to hurt you. I want to get you to a doctor."

Her eyes were filled with fear, but she nodded.

"My name's Jasper, ma'am and I'm a married man with a family. You have no reason to fear me. I have a blanket to wrap you in, but first, Ma'am I got to try and stop the bleedin' in between your legs."

Her eyes grew larger.

"Ma'am, I'm just going to press these bandages there, that's all." She slowly nodded.

He applied the bandages as gently as he could and then wrapped her in the blanket. The fear in her eyes lessened.

"My husband, Orrin?" She asked in a quiet, hoarse voice.

"I'm afraid he's gone, ma'am."

She quietly sobbed and tears flowed from her eyes.

"Ma'am, I have to ask you who did this?"

"Five men." She wiped her hand across her face streaking the dirt covering her cheeks.

"Did one of them wear a black vest and a brown hat?"

She nodded, her eyes wide.

"And a big knife on his belt?"

"Yes."

"I'm hunting these men for murdering some of my family and a young woman in Cassidy County."

"Your wife and children?!"

"No, thank God. They killed my pa and my brothers."

"I'm sorry."

He looked at her sad eyes. "We'll share sorrow." Jasper stood. "Ma'am, I'm going to have to lay your husband back here."

She nodded. "Can you put Orrin in my arms?"

"Uh, ma'am, that might not be such a pleasant thing to do."

"I know, but I *need* to hold him."

Jasper thought about what he would do if Gale died. "Yes, ma'am. I understand."

Jasper lifted the body and moved it as gently as he could. He carefully laid the man next to his wife. She turned and put her arms around him. This act deeply touched Jasper.

"Thank you."

"Yes, ma'am."

"Please call me Beth."

"All right, Beth. I'm going to hitch my horse to the wagon. I'll try to make the ride as easy as I can, but I've got to get you to the doctor in Kentville."

Beth nodded.

Jasper tried his best to keep the ride as smooth as possible but he could hear Beth whimper in pain, though he didn't know if her cries were from pain or from sorrow. After some time he stopped to check on the bleeding between her legs, a task painfully uncomfortable for him.

"Don't be embarrassed, Jasper. I know you're only tryin' to take care of me."

He looked at her ivory pale face. "I can't help it, ma'am. I'm respectful of womankind." He moved the makeshift bandage which was soaked in blood. "Beth, I can't stop the bleedin' because it's from the inside. I have to go faster. We need to get you to the doctor."

Beth grimaced. "All right."

Jasper jumped onto the wagon seat and urged Coal on.

Kent County Deputy Sheriff, Mac Twittle, stood motionless in thick bushes looking at the man in the wagon. He recognized Jasper Lee from the wanted posters he'd tacked up outside the sheriff's office the day before. The wagon stopped on the road just after Twittle relieved himself. For an instant Twittle toyed with the idea of trying to take Lee by himself, but he knew that would mean a quick death. Besides, the sheriff said Lee needed to be taken alive. The governor wanted him to stand trial. He decided the best thing to do was to follow Lee and then find help.

Dusk was crawling over the land by the time Jasper neared Kentville. He had thrown his usual caution to the wind for Beth's sake, but her muted agony still tore his heart out. Because of what Harry told him about the governor's men looking for him he knew he couldn't just drive the wagon down main street, so he pulled Coal to a stop and turned to Beth. His heart stopped. She looked dead.

"Beth?"

Her eyes fluttered open. "I'm still here, Jasper." Her words were barely loud enough to reach his ears.

"We're just outside of Kentville. Do you know a doctor here?"

"Yes, I go to Doctor Scoville."

"It's late so we better go to his house."

"His office is in his house. It's the big white one on the east edge of town. Just keep to the east and you'll see it."

A quarter mile passed before Jasper spotted the house. He pulled up and the sign read, "Dr. Amos Scoville and Family." He jumped off the wagon, banged on the door with his fist. A commotion and loud voices sounded from within. The door opened and a tall, older man with a kind face appeared.

"Doctor Scoville?"

"Yes, what's the problem?"

"I brought a woman who's in a real bad way. I found her and her husband on the wagon road. Her husband's been murdered and she's been beaten and violated."

The doctor pushed by Jasper. "Who is she?"

"I just know her by Beth."

"Oh my God! Beth Harris!" The doctor sprinted to the wagon and climbed on. He knelt by Beth's head, gently moving her husband's body. "Beth," he whispered. "It's me Doctor Scoville."

Beth's hand reached up and grasped the doctor's arm. "Thank God," she said.

The doctor turned to Jasper. "Help me get her inside."

A woman in a long dressing gown came outside. "Amos! What's the matter?"

"It's Beth Harris, Doris. Get the long care room ready."

"Oh, my dear." Doris hurried off.

Jasper and the doctor carried Beth into the house and laid her on a bed in a room in the back of the house.

"When did you find her?" Doctor Scoville asked.

"About three hours ago. I tried to stop the bleedin', but I'm afraid it's comin' from the inside."

Doris came in with instruments and hot water

"All right," the doctor said. He pulled on a sleeved apron and tied the strings at his waist. "Please wait outside. I'll need to ask you some more questions in a while."

Jasper turned to step out, but Beth grabbed his hand.

"Thank you for taking care of me, Jasper." Her voice was a breathless whisper.

"I'm glad I found you, Beth."

Chapter Fifteen

STAN BARSTOW WATCHED Doc Evanson rinse the flesh and blood off the bullets he'd dug out of the bodies of Deputy Coy Jeffers and the prisoner, Rich Delton. He lifted the metal tray and examined the lead slugs.

"The bullets that came out of Delton's body are .44-40 caliber. A pretty common round. The slugs that came out of Coy's body are .41 Remington. Not a common round. Not common at all."

"How do you know this stuff, Stan?"

"Just like you know medicine, I know crime and the tools used to commit crimes."

"What are you gonna do now?"

"I'm going to go home, have some dinner and get a good night's sleep. Then I'll leave for Fort Hurley early in the morning, get some warrants and head to Kentville."

"You'd better be careful there, Stan. These killers obviously targeted Delton. That probably means more than just the two of them are involved."

Stan nodded. "I know. I'll be careful."

Jasper paced back and forth in the Scoville's living room. The doctor had been working on Beth for almost two hours. Fury kept building in Jasper making him hell bent on killing the men who did this to her.

They had killed seven people and raped five women that he knew of. They were dangerous and needed to be scrubbed from this Earth.

The door to Beth's room opened and Doctor Scoville came out. He looked exhausted.

"How is she, Doc?"

"I don't know if she's going to make it. She's lost so much blood, it's going to be close."

"But you did get the bleedin' stopped, didn't you?"

Scoville looked at Jasper with narrowing eyes. "Yes, I did. I had to perform surgery on her, but I got the bleeding stopped and repaired her injuries. But I have a question for you."

"What's that?"

"You're Jasper Lee aren't you?"

"Yes, sir."

"Why does an outlaw like you care about a lady like Beth?"

"Outlaw? What are you talking about? I'm no outlaw."

"Somebody thinks you are. There are posters all over town saying you're wanted for the murder of thirteen men."

Jasper felt his temples pounding. "I might have killed thirteen men but they were part of the gang that murdered my pa and brothers in cold blood, then raped and tortured an innocent young woman to death in Cassidy County. They murdered two people and raped two women in Indian Country and did this to Beth. I'm no outlaw, Doctor, but I'm damn sure the man who is going to bring these scum to natural justice and wipe them off the face of the earth." Jasper found himself breathing hard.

"Are you talking about that scoundrel Bart Moore and his gang?"

"Yes, sir. I figure there's five of them left and those five killed Beth's husband and attacked her. I believe they're here in Kentville now."

"Do they know you brought Beth here?"

"No, sir."

"Well, Mr. Lee, if you want my advice you'll get out of town. Bart Moore is the governor's nephew and Cornell Norris is not about to let you or anyone else hurt him. I suspect he's the one behind the warrant for your arrest. They know you're coming and just put the posters up around here. If they catch you, you'll hang."

"I've never run from anything and I'm not startin' now. I'm going to stay out on the edge of town until I figure out where Moore and his gang are and then I'll make my move."

"I believe you're going to find yourself vastly outnumbered in more ways than one. This town, this county and most of the territory are owned by Governor Norris. You're asking for trouble, but it's your funeral, Mr. Lee."

"Thank you for the advice, Doctor, but I don't think the Governor owns as much of this territory he thinks he does. Now, I have a question for you."

"What's that?"

"With Beth's husband dead is she going to have enough money to recover?"

"Probably not. They had a small ranch outside of town a ways but they were just getting started. It's not worth much, but don't worry. I'll take good care of her."

Jasper pulled a poke out his pocket, retrieved two twenty dollar gold coins and handed them to the doctor. "This should help her out a little."

"You don't have to do this, Mr. Lee. We'll take care of her."

"She's a brave and tough young lady who loved her husband. I think everyone should help her. I'm just doing my part. You'll take care of her husband?"

The doctor nodded.

Jasper picked up his hat and headed for the door.

"Mr. Lee...Jasper..."

Jasper half turned and looked at the doctor. "Yes, sir?"

"Beth was pregnant. I couldn't save the baby."

Jasper turned to the door, pulling his hat down hard onto his forehead.

The night air felt cool as he headed for Coal. The thought of Beth's loss brought up the tears his father had taught him not to cry. He unhitched Coal and rode around the outskirts of Kentville getting a feel for the town and looking for any trace of Moore and his gang. He heard the sound of a saloon piano and the buzz of men enjoying themselves. He eased closer.

His eye caught movement in the shadows to his left. As he turned to get a better look he heard boots to his right and rear. Jasper reached for his guns.

"This is the Sheriff, Lee. You're surrounded. Don't move or you'll die."

He heard several guns cock and realized there were more men than he could see.

"Raise your hands high."

Jasper complied.

"Dismount slow and easy, Lee, or the first thing we'll shoot is your fine lookin' horse."

Jasper lifted his left leg over the saddle horn and slid off Coal on the right side. Men rushed forward and grabbed his arms, taking his gun belt and Bowie knife. His hands were manacled behind his back.

Coal snorted and did a jittery dance. "Easy, Coal...easy, boy," Jasper said.

"Well, mister gunfighter, I'm Sheriff Morey Lock and it looks like we got the bulge on you," the sheriff chortled.

A short plump deputy walked up to the sheriff. "That's mighty fine horse flesh ya got there, Lee. Hey, Sheriff, since Lee won't be needin' his horse no more how about lettin' me have him as a bonus for findin' him?"

"Have at it, Mac."

"I wouldn't do that if I were you," Jasper said in a low voice.

"Well, you're not me, Lee, so you can go to hell." The deputy stepped to Coal and put his foot in the stirrup. He swung his leg over the saddle and started to settle in...Coal exploded.

Men scattered as Coal bucked, kicked, twisted and turned. The deputy screamed like a banshee and hung on with both hands. His body was a blur as it jerked and spun on the saddle. Then he was airborne, flying head first into the tall wall of the Kentville Hotel. His head hit with a crunch sounding like a crushed eggshell and the body flopped on the ground with a dull thud.

Jasper smiled with satisfaction as Coal galloped into the night. Lock and the others rushed over to the body.

Lock then came back and glared at Jasper. "What in the hell did you do, Lee?"

"Whaddya mean?" Jasper was fighting hard to suppress a smile. "I told him not to do it and he told me to go to hell. Guess he had it all figured out."

"Goddammit!" The sheriff's jaws were so tight, the curse barely made it out. "C'mon, let's get this son of a bitch to the jail."

"Sheriff! What are we going to do about Mac?" A deputy asked.

"Do I have to do everything around here? You take care of it!" He shoved Jasper's back. "Let's go."

Chapter Sixteen

BLACK FEATHER ROSE WITH A START as he heard a horse gallop into the village. He rushed outside and could just make out Coal in the early morning glow beginning to light the eastern sky.

"Coal! Come here, boy!"

The big horse trotted to him, his head moving up and down with a quiet nicker.

"Easy." Black Feather took Coal's reins from the saddle horn and rubbed Coal's nose and cheeks. He whispered soothing words and patted the lathered neck until the big horse calmed, then led him to the lake so he could drink.

Rain Water's steps were soft, but Black Feather always recognized them. "Where is Fire Hawk?"

"I do not know, Mother, but he must be in trouble." He un-cinched the saddle and set it on the grass. "Coal has come to take me to him."

"I fear for him, Black Feather. There are too many enemies for him to face alone."

Wind Runner and Claw Of The Eagle came running.

"Is Fire Hawk hurt?" Wind Runner asked.

"I do not know, but I must prepare for a long ride to find my brother."

"We are going with you, Black Feather," Wind Runner said.

"It is not necessary for you to go."

"Yes it is," Claw Of The Eagle folded his arms across his chest. "Fire Hawk treated our wives as his sisters. That makes him our brother."

Black Feather looked at the two warriors. "Then we will go together. Go prepare to ride and to fight. We'll leave as soon as Coal is rested."

"I will send a rider to tell Gale Jasper is in trouble," Rain Water said. Then she opened her arms to the men. "Warriors, may the spirits guide you...bring my son home."

"Wake up, Lee! You have a visitor," the jailer shouted.

Jasper sat up on his cot. A short man with horned rimmed spectacles stepped up to the iron bars. He looked no older than sixteen years. An over-sized broadcloth shirt was stuffed into baggy nankeen trousers that hit his leg just above the ankle, showing off shoes that even an expert cobbler wouldn't have been able to fix. The state of a suit coat that barely buttoned over his thin frame matched the condition of the shoes.

"Hello, Mr. Lee. I'm Willis Harwick, lawyer and counselor at law. I hear you've been looking for a legal counsel but no one will take your case."

"I don't mean any offense, Mr. Harwick, but are you sure you're old enough to be a lawyer?"

"Why yes, sir. I'm twenty-eight years old and a graduate of Harvard Law School. I was admitted to the bar nine months ago. I know that doesn't indicate a wealth of experience but I assure you no one would fight harder for your rights."

Jasper looked the young man over and remembered the words of Hawk. *Do not judge every one by how they look. The outwardly meek often have great strength and courage in their hearts. Trust those with clear eyes and clean tongue...*

"Well, at least you're honest about it. What's your fee?"

"Uh, honestly, Mr. Lee I haven't really thought about it."

"What do you usually charge?"

Willis glanced at his feet and interlaced his fingers in front of him so tight Jasper thought he might break them off. He took a deep breath. "To be perfectly honest with you, Mr. Lee, you would be my first client."

Jasper's eyebrows raised as he breathed in and released a deep breath. He considered Harwick's words for a moment, thinking the man's resume was a might short, but his heart was true. "One last question. Do you know what's goin' on here?"

"Why, yes, you've been charged with thirteen counts of murder."

"Where did these murders supposedly take place?"

"I don't know yet. Somewhere in Kent County, I assume."

"Actually, the gunfight took place in Cassidy County and only one person knows who killed those men."

"If that's true it presents significant legal issues for the prosecution to overcome."

"It really doesn't because I'm bein' railroaded. If you take my case you'll be up against a corrupt government. It could get dangerous."

Willis straightened his back and a resolve and fire lit his eyes. "Well, sir, I became a lawyer to do some good in this world. I've heard rumors about the corruption here. I would be honored to fight such monstrosity on your behalf."

"Okay, Mr. Harwick, you're hired." Jasper reached down, loosened the top of his moccasin and removed a strip of cowhide holding gold coins. He counted five coins and handed them through the bars. "That should get us started."

"Yes, sir!"

"Willis…"

"Yes, sir?"

"Call me Jasper."

"Thank you, Jasper. "Willis reached through the bars and shook Jasper's hand. "You won't be sorry."

"Here's an extra forty dollars. Get yourself fixed up with some decent clothes. I want my lawyer at least dressed as well as the lawyer against me."

Willis' face tightened and flushed as he fought back tears. "Thank you, Jasper.

Two days later, Stan rode into Kentville. The warmth as the sun climbed into the sky replaced the chill he felt when he left Fort Hurley in the early morning. In his inside vest pocket he carried two "John Doe" warrants that authorized the arrest of the men matching the description of the killers.

He pulled up at Mrs. Colson's Boarding House and Restaurant, dismounted and went inside, taking a table at the window with a view of the Governor's office.

A teen aged girl walked up to him. "What can I get you, sir?"

"I'd like some steak and eggs with coffee, please."

"Breakfast comes with some of mom's fried potatoes, if that's okay?"

"That would be fine."

"I'll get the coffee right up for you."

Stan leaned back in his chair and stretched his legs. The girl set his coffee on the table. He took a sip and watched the people and traffic on the street. He was hoping to confront the suspects in front of the governor's office to minimize the chance of gun play. The governor's men taking on the US Marshal in front of so many people would be bad publicity for the politician.

Ten minutes later the girl brought his breakfast. "Did you hear the news about the big trial?"

"No, can't say I have."

"They caught that gunfighter, Jasper Lee. They say he killed thirteen men."

"Hmm, that's interesting." Stan picked up his fork. "Thanks for the news, young lady."

"You're welcome, sir. Enjoy your breakfast."

Stan ate his breakfast thinking about Jasper Lee. He found it interesting that a case had been made when as far as he knew no investigation had been done. As he sipped on another cup of coffee, the governor's buggy rolled down the street with his escorts. Stan stood and dropped two dollars on the table, then he walked out into the street.

He approached the governor's carriage but two men stepped in front of him. They matched the descriptions Bernie had given him. "I need to see the governor."

"Yeah, doesn't everyone. Make an appointment," the man with the scar sneered.

The governor stepped out of the coach.

"Governor!" Stan yelled.

The man with the scar cocked back to throw a punch, but a kick to the groin dropped him to the ground. The second man grabbed the grip of his pistol but before he could clear leather he was staring down the barrel of Stan's Colt.

"United States Marshal! Don't move!"

The man let go of his gun and raised his hands.

"What's the meaning of this!" The governor roared.

"I'm Stan Barstow, United States Marshal." He knelt and manacled the hands of the man with the scar who lay moaning in the fetal position. "I'm arresting this man for the murder of a deputy town marshal." Stan removed the man's gun and saw it was a .41 Remington.

"Murder, why t-that's preposterous!" the governor stammered.

Stan showed the governor the warrant. "Not hardly, Governor."

"Well, these warrants have no names, only descriptions. This is hardly proper."

"You'll have to take that up with Judge Abramson of the federal district court, sir. For now these men are under arrest." He turned to the other man. "I need to take a look at your gun."

The man hesitated.

"Do as the marshal says, Carlos," the governor ordered. "We have nothing to hide."

Using two fingers, Carlos pulled his Army Colt and handed it to Stan.

Stan looked on the barrel and saw it was a 44-40 caliber. "You're under arrest, too, Carlos." He turned the man around and tied his hands with a leather tong, one of several he carried in his back pocket.

Norris puffed out his chest and stepped toward Stan. "I don't take kindly to you arresting my two best men."

"And I don't take too damn kindly to my deputy being shot in the back!"

The governor's face flushed bright red. A crowd had formed and he looked around and then straightened his coat and tie. "I'm sure this is all a mistake and we will get it rectified. Don't worry men, my lawyers will have you out of jail before your cots are warm."

Stan helped the man he kicked stand up. "What's your name?"

"Reece Burton."

"Well Reece, you're under arrest for the murder of Deputy Coy Jeffers."

"Carlos, what's your last name."

"McElroy."

"You're under arrest for the murder of Rich Delton. Get on your horses." Stan helped both men get mounted, tied their hands to their saddle horns then led their horses to his. He took a rope and hitched the horses in tow with his, mounted and headed out of town at a fast trot.

As he headed out Sheriff Lock rode up to him.

"What's goin' on?"

"I'm United States Marshal Stan Barstow. These men are my prisoners."

"You're shittin' me!"

"No, I'm not."

"Well, bud, I think you just bought yourself a whole heap of trouble."

"Thanks for the tip." Stan spurred his horse past the sheriff. When he looked back the sheriff was headed for the governor's office.

The governor was already in a bad mood when his nephew came through the back door to his office.

"What in hell are you doing here? I told you to stay at the ranch."

"Your foreman kicked me off the ranch just because a couple of cowboys don't like me."

"Goddamn it! Things are going to hell around here! Can't you even..."

A knock at the front door interrupted Norris' tirade at Moore.

"Who is it?"

"It's Sheriff Lock, Governor."

"Get in here, Morey."

Lock stepped in and closed the door.

"I take it you saw the new US Marshal taking Carlos and Reece out of town."

"Yes, sir. I did."

"This is serious. Those two know too much and that marshal is too damn smart for his own good."

"Whaddya want to do?" Lock took off his hat and wiped his forehead.

"The marshal can't make it back to Fort Hurley with Carlos and Reece. You got enough spare men to take care of that?"

"No, sir, I don't. Not for a job like that. The most I have for it is two men."

Moore rested his fists on the governor's desk. "My men and I can take care of it, Uncle."

The governor leaned toward the outlaw. "Get your hands off my desk."

Bart jumped back and looked down at the governor.

Norris stared back until Moore looked down at the floor and shuffled his feet.

The governor turned to Lock. "Morey, get your men and meet back here. Bart, you do the same."

"Don't worry, Uncle Cornell, I'll take care of it."

"You're not doing a damn thing except staying here with me where I can keep an eye on you."

"Uncle, this is my kind of job. I can do it right."

The governor thought for a minute. "How many men do you have?"

"Four."

"All right, Morey tell your men Bart is in charge. Bart, I want you to kill all three, the marshal, Reece and Carlos. Make it look like some bandits ambushed them. I just don't want any witnesses. You understand?"

"Yeah, I understand."

"Set the ambush just this side of the Ft. Hurley junction. That's far enough away so it won't be able to be traced back here. Do a good job of burying the bodies."

"I'll go get my men," Moore said as he started toward the back door.

"And tell the men they'll get an extra fifty dollars if the job is done right."

"Yes, sir, Uncle Cornell." Moore rushed out of the office.

"Morey," the governor scribbled a note for the judge, "Before you get your men, go give this to the judge. I want to make sure the trial starts today. We gotta keep the folks thinking about Jasper Lee while we finish the rest of our business."

Lock took the note. "I'll take care of it."

Chapter Seventeen

PEOPLE CROWDED THE COURTROOM and Cornell Norris felt a flash of nervousness that he quickly suppressed.

"Court is now in session!" Judge Iverson announced. "The case is the Territory versus Jasper Lee, Criminal Docket Number 17."

The new lawyer, Harwick, fiddled with papers on the table.

"The selected jurors will take their place in the jury box."

A grumble of disapproval flitted through the crowd.

"Order! Order!" Iverson banged his gavel.

Harwick rose to his feet. "Your Honor, I must object to this procedure. I haven't had an opportunity to question the prospective jurors and my client hasn't even entered a plea!"

"Objection overruled, Mr. Harwick. I figured Mr. Lee will enter a plea of not guilty and I know a good jury when I see one."

"Your Honor, the question isn't whether or not the jury is a good one, but whether or not it is a fair one."

"Are you questioning *my* integrity, counsel?"

Harwick took a deep breath. "Based on your last two decisions, yes, sir, I am...for the record."

An uneasy silence descended on the courtroom. Harwick was good. Too good. He'd have to be eliminated. That meant they needed time to take care of the problem.

Iverson shuffled papers on the bench.

The uncomfortable feeling that the people around him were starting to fold under pressure settled in the pit of the governor's stomach.

Harwick apparently noticed the judge's condition too, because he drilled in. "Your Honor! We can't start the trial now. I haven't had a chance to investigate this case."

"There shouldn't be much dispute about the facts, Mr. Harwick."

The young lawyer's voice deepened and he leaned forward, his jaw jutting towards the judge. "On the contrary, your Honor, we dispute all of the facts and challenge the venue of the court to hear this case. We further object to the unconstitutional procedures this court seems bent on following."

"Mr. Harwick, you can't challenge the venue of the case when the prosecutor hasn't had a chance to present evidence on venue."

"I certainly can challenge the process of these proceedings and the failure to impanel a jury without the proper procedures guaranteed by the United States Constitution. I demand this trial be stayed so that I may bring an appeal to the federal court."

The judge slid his eyes over to the governor and Cornell nodded his head just enough for Iverson to get the message.

"All right, Mr. Harwick, I'll grant your motion for a stay. You have until 9:00 Thursday morning. Court adjourned!"

When the crowd had cleared the governor strode into the judge's chambers followed by the prosecutor and the sheriff.

"I don't like this, Cornell," the judge complained. "I didn't expect Lee to be able to get a lawyer to represent him."

"I must admit that runt Harwick wasn't doing too bad a job," the prosecutor said.

"Shut up, both of you. I wanted to give him some time so he would go to the federal court in Fort Hurley."

"Letting him appeal to the federal court is not a good idea." Iverson's voice cracked like a thirteen year old boy just hitting puberty.

"He won't make it to any damn federal court. Thursday you'll be able to run the trial without any bothersome objections."

"Cornell, how many people can you keep on killing without blowing up everything we worked for?"

"Don't get skittish on me, Rance. We've run into a little bad luck and we just have to tie up loose ends."

Chapter Eighteen

AFTER THEY GOT ABOUT A MILE from Kentville, Stan rearranged the caravan so his prisoners were in front of him. This made it so he could keep an eye on his charges, but it also slowed them down. He retied their hands in front of them but ran a line from both men back to his saddle horn. The prisoners were in no hurry to get to Fort Hurley and Stan had to snap a lariat on the rear of their horses to keep them moving at a decent pace.

"Hey, Marshal. I need to piss," Carlos McElroy complained after they had been riding for four hours.

Stan stood in his stirrups and looked around. They were in a small ravine surrounded by rocks and boulders with a few trees and brush, about a half a mile from the Fort Hurley junction.

"Okay, we'll take a break here." Stan dismounted and wrapped his reins around a low branch, then loosened the line on Carlos. "You can go one at a time."

The prisoner slid off and Stan stood by holding the line.

"What's up, Marshal? You some kind of sissy boy that you gotta watch us piss?" Carlos sneered.

"I can fix it so you can piss in your pants, if that's want you want."

"Yeah, yeah, you bastard." Carlos took care of business and then climbed back on his horse.

Stan retied the line and loosened the rope on Reece. "Okay, your turn."

Reece got off his horse. "I need some more line."

"Piss right there."

"Look, bunghole..." Blood and lung blew out of Reece's chest before he could finish. In the second it took for Stan to realize that

Reece had been shot, another bullet smashed into Carlos' leg. He dropped off his horse screaming a string of curses in Spanish.

Stan jumped behind his horse just avoiding a hail of gunfire. The horse danced wildly from side to side but Stan managed to grab his rifle. With one quick move he sliced the line tied to Carlos, took hold of the downed outlaw's arm and pulled him toward the nearest boulder. A torrent of snapping bullets and ricochets bouncing off the ground raised a choking dust. Bullet fragments sprayed rock shards as Stan dragged Carlo's dead weight around the boulder. He stumbled.

"Damn!" Stan said under his breath. He looked at his side and saw the blood oozing through his shirt.

"Son of a bitch!" Carlos grimaced as he squeezed his hands around his blood-soaked thigh. "How could those bastards miss you and hit me and Reece?!"

"Because they're shooting at all of us." Stan fired at a puff of gun smoke.

Carlos' eyes grew wide. "That no good, goddamn, bunghole!"

Stan shot toward the ambushers but couldn't tell if he hit anything. "Who?"

"The governor, that's who. Give me a gun so I can shoot back!"

"I don't think so." Stan fired several more shots hoping to keep the attacker's heads down.

"Then we're goin' to die."

"I guess we all gotta go sometime."

Stan was trying to keep the attackers at bay but he knew they were closing in. He looked at Carlos and could see the fear in his eyes. For a fleeting moment he thought about giving him a gun but then he thought of Coy, his murdered deputy, and thought better of it. He loaded his last eight rounds into his Henry rifle.

"This is bullshit, Marshal."

Stan saw a man flanking on the right side, drew a bead and fired. The man collapsed.

"I finally nailed one!"

He saw two coming at him from the left but suddenly one dropped hard and a gunshot reached his ears. Then he heard more shots and Indian war cries.

"Well, well, Carlos. I think we just got some help!"

Black Feather sounded a war hoop and galloped toward the ambush. A gunman turned towards him but before the man could aim his pistol, Black Feather's shot tore through his face blowing half of it into a bright red spray. Another turned to run and Black Feather shot him in the back, sprawling him against a boulder.

Wind Runner charged into the middle of the attackers' position. One man jumped on a horse and Wind Runner used his own horse as a ram, knocking the other horse to the ground. The warrior jumped down and sank his tomahawk into the other rider's skull. Then within a breath he leapt over a large rock toward a man raising a rifle at him. Wind Runner knocked the gun aside and grabbed the last man by the hair. The scream trying to come out was cut short by the hack that almost cut the man's head off.

They heard a galloping horse and turned to see a man wearing a brown hat and black vest riding away. Claw Of The Eagle took a few shots from his high ground position but the rider was too far away.

Wind Runner started for his horse.

"No, Wind Runner. We must see if Stan Barstow is all right."

Stan wrapped the bandage he tore from Carlos' shirt around the prisoner's thigh. He looked up when three riders leading a fourth horse came around the boulder. Relief released the breath he'd been holding. "Many thanks, Black Feather. I didn't think we were going to make it there for a minute."

Black Feather slid off his horse. "You are wounded, Stan Barstow."

"Oh, I'll be all right." Stan tried to stand but his knees hit the ground and the air left his lungs with a grunt. "Be still. We will bandage you and take you to Fort Hurley."

Stan was thinking it might be a good idea to take Black Feather's advice. "What are you men doing out here?"

"Looking for Fire Hawk."

"Fire Hawk?"

"You know him as Jasper Lee. He is our brother."

"Your brother! That Jasper Lee sure is an interesting man." Stan grimaced as Black Feather worked on his side. "Jasper's in jail in Kentville, standing trial for murder."

"And that's a bunch of bullshit!" Carlos yelled.

"What do you mean, Carlos?" Stan frowned.

"It's a rigged deal, set up by the governor to take the heat off of his nephew."

"How do you know this?"

"Who do you think ordered me and Reece to kill Delton?"

Stan felt his face flush.

"Sorry about your deputy, Marshal. He really didn't deserve to die but he was doing his job too well and Reece wasn't right in the head…a natural born killer, Reece was."

"Carlos, if you'll testify about this I'll recommend leniency from the court."

"For what? Life in prison? No thanks, Marshal. I'll testify just for payback on that son of a bitch, Norris. I can give the goods on a bunch of others, too."

Black Feather put his hand on Stan's shoulder. "How much time do we have to get to Kentville before they hang our brother?"

"Since they're doing a trial, probably a couple of days," Stan answered. "But that's not for sure. I'm thinking trying to take all the governor's men with just the four of us isn't very smart. We need to get to Fort Hurley and see what help we can get but I need one of you to ride to Arlington and tell your brother's wife he's in the Kent County jail."

"I'll go." Claw Of The Eagle mounted his horse and galloped off.

Stan's side burned like fire but he was feeling better when Black Feather helped him to his feet. "Let's ride then."

Chapter Nineteen

THE NEXT MORNING Judge Abramson finished signing the warrants for everyone identified by Carlos McElroy including the sheriff, the judge and the prosecutor of Kent County as well as the Territorial Governor, Cornell Norris.

"Well, Marshal, it looks like you've got yourself a good case against the governor and his conspirators on some very serious crimes."

"Yes, sir. I'm going to need help making these arrests, Judge. I would like you to appoint Black Feather and Wind Runner as deputy marshals."

The judge sat back in his chair and considered the Indians standing in front of him.

"Do you gentlemen understand the laws of the United States?"

A grim smile crossed Black Feather's mouth. "We do, Judge, but we do not like them. Your laws depend on whose enforcing them."

"And your laws don't have that problem?"

"Our laws are based on the natural law and guidance from the spirits, not the greed of men."

"If you say so, Black Feather, but like it or not, when your clan signed the treaty the laws of this territory and the United States became your laws also. If you accept the commission as a deputy marshal you must act according to those laws. In this territory, under my supervision, that means you'll do so honestly and fairly. Now I think you can do that, but I need you to tell me you will."

Black Feather looked at Wind Runner who shrugged and nodded his head.

"We will, Judge."

The judge stood up and pulled a bible out of his desk drawer. "Raise your right hands."

After the two new deputies were commissioned Stan told the judge about Claw Of The Eagle. The judge wrote out a commission giving Stan the authority to give the oath to his third deputy.

"Bailiff!"

"Yes, your honor."

"Go to Captain Anthony and ask him to the court."

"Right away, sir."

A few minutes later the captain entered the courtroom. "You ask for me, Your Honor?"

"Yes, Captain. Marshal, do you have enough men to arrest all the people you have warrants for?"

"Just myself and two, maybe three, deputies."

"Captain, I request a squad of soldiers accompany the marshal and his deputies to Kentville to assist in the arrest of a group of suspects. One of those suspects is the territorial governor."

The captain's face lit up. "I'll lead the squad myself, sir."

"Good man. Well, Marshal, get the show on the road."

"Yes, sir and thank you."

Willis surprised himself when he made it into the saddle on the second try.

"Are you sure you want to do this?" Doctor Scoville asked.

"I have to, Amos. My client is being railroaded to a hanging and it's my duty to fight for him."

"You do realize your life is in danger, don't you?"

A tremble crawled up Willis' spine. "Yes, I do."

"Do you have a gun?"

"I wouldn't know how to use it if I did."

"All right, Willis. Walnut is a good horse. My daughter learned to ride on her and Walnut took care of her. She'll take care of you too."

"I hope so, Amos." With that, Willis snapped the reins on the horse and started down the road to Fort Hurley, his head and upper body bouncing up and down, left and right precariously in the saddle.

Four hours later Willis' back and butt were causing him great pain and discomfort but filled with his sense of duty and mission he wouldn't stop and rest. The Fort Hurley junction was in sight and a little relief flowed through him for he was over half way to his destination.

Suddenly a heavy blow slammed into the side of his head. He tried to hang on the saddle but the horse stopped in its tracks and Willis was thrown to the ground. The world went black.

Stan and his troop had been riding for three hours. They were a quarter mile from the Hurley junction when they heard a shot.

"Keep a sharp eye," the captain ordered. "And form a skirmish line. Forward Ho!"

They rode cautiously until they reached the junction. Stan and Captain Anthony stopped and surveyed the area. "Black Feather, you and Wind Runner scout ahead," Stan said.

They nodded and began to weave their horses through the trees until they disappeared.

"Marshal!" Wind Runner called.

Stan and the squad hurried toward the sound of his deputy's voice. Next to a chestnut colored horse Wind Runner bent over a body.

The captain ordered the squad to set up a perimeter.

Stan slid off his horse and kneeling next to the body he recognized the new lawyer from Kentville. A deep furrow creased the young man's scalp but he was still alive.

A soldier retrieved bandages and water and cleaned up the wound.

Stan checked through the lawyer's saddle bags. He found court papers and immediately realized the lawyer, Willis Harwick, represented Jasper Lee.

Black Feather approached.

"Two men shot him from that hill." Black Feather held up a spent .32 Winchester Center Fire cartridge. "I saw the tracks of two horses. One had a cracked shoe on the left front hoof. I also saw the boot mark of the shooter. A piece of the right heel is missing. We must have scared them off. I can catch up to them if you want."

"Go ahead, but just follow them so we can identify them later. We'll get Mr. Harwick here to the doctor in Kentville."

Black Feather mounted his horse and galloped off.

Stan heard a moan and knelt by the injured man. "Mr. Harwick?"

The lawyer's eyes opened and filled with fear.

"It's all right, sir. I'm Stan Barstow, US Marshal."

Harwick tried to sit up but fell backwards onto the arm Stan threw out to catch him. "What happened to me?"

"You were ambushed and shot in the head, but it's just a deep gash. I suspect you're going to have one helluva headache, otherwise you'll be okay."

Harwick struggled into a sitting position. "I've got to get to Fort Hurley and try to stop the trial. They're going to hang Jasper Lee if I don't."

"Did you get a stay on the trial to make an appeal?"

"Yes, for two days."

Stan thought for a minute. "Do you know any doctors in Kentville?"

"Amos Scoville is a doctor and good friend."

"Will he let you stay at his house?"

"Of course, but why?"

"We'll fix up a litter and get you to the good doctor."

"No! I have to get to Fort Hurley!"

"Easy Mr. Harwick, there won't be any hanging anytime soon. I have warrants for the arrest of the governor and his friends, including the judge and the prosecutor. You don't need to go to Fort Hurley."

Willis touched his head. "Then we need to get to Kentville with all possible speed. I can ride Marshal."

"Mr. Harwick, the minute you try to stand you'll fall flat on your face. That bullet didn't kill you but your wound isn't one to be taken lightly."

The captain pointed to two soldiers. "You men make a litter for this gentleman. Make it quick."

"Thanks, Captain," Stan said. "I hope we're not running out of time."

Chapter Twenty

GALE STOOD UPRIGHT IN THE WAGON. Burt Ashton was bringing more folks into town. Micah, Sean and Claw Of The Eagle were on horseback next to her.

"By golly, looks like everyone is here," Micah said.

Gail turned to the crowd that had gathered in front of her. "Thank you all for coming to support Jasper. We have to get moving because we don't know where things stand with his trial." She looked back into the bed of the wagon. "Are you ready, Mr. Dolan?"

"I am, Mrs. Lee. Ready to avenge my daughter."

Gale sat down and looked at Jessica Dolan sitting next to her. "You ready, Jessica?"

Jessica nodded. "More than ready."

Gale looked at Megan, Brenden and Abbey standing with Rain Water and knew her children would be safe until her return. She hoped she could say the same for her husband. "Children, you behave for Rain Water."

"We will, Ma," Megan replied with authority.

"Thank you, Rain Water."

"Go Gale. Use your fire to bring my son home."

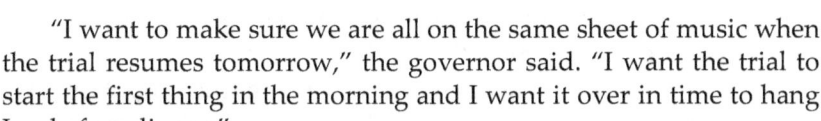

"I want to make sure we are all on the same sheet of music when the trial resumes tomorrow," the governor said. "I want the trial to start the first thing in the morning and I want it over in time to hang Lee before dinner."

Jeremy Sykes, the prosecutor, cleared his throat. "With Harwick out of the picture things should go smoothly."

"I'll make that determination, Jeremy," Judge Iverson said. Cornell noticed a bit of curtness in the judge's reply. "Since Harwick was involved there is a record being made. It has to be plausible."

"He's no longer involved," the governor said flatly.

"That may be true," the judge said, "but he was a lawyer and a graduate of Harvard. Even if he's just missing, someone may look into it."

"All right. I don't care what you have to do, just meet my time table. Don't worry too much about the trial. People may not like the process, but they always love a good hanging."

A knock at the back door interrupted the governor. He motioned to Lock to check it out.

Lock carefully opened the door and Bart Moore burst in.

"Where the hell have you been?!" the governor roared.

"Layin' low."

"Where's everyone else?"

"Dead."

Cornell grabbed Bart by the front of his shirt. "Don't tell me you screwed this up too! What happened?"

"W...w...we had them. I know Reece and Carlos are dead... I...I saw them drop, but before I could make sure the marshal was dead we got attacked by Indians!"

"Indians? What in the hell are you talking about? There are no hostile Indians in this area!"

"Well, they sure as hell were hostile to us!"

"Are you telling me that marshal is still alive?"

"No, I ain't sayin' that. He was hit. I saw the blood on him. He's probably dead, I just ain't as sure about him as I am about Reece and Carlos."

"Goddamn it!" Cornell shoved his nephew and Bart banged hard against the wall. "I should've known better than to trust you to get the job done."

Bart rubbed at the back of his head and glared at his uncle. "It wasn't my fault. We set a good ambush and had 'em, but those damn Indians came out of nowhere."

Norris could see his nephew was telling the truth about that. He wasn't so sure about the rest.

"With Reece and Carlos dead the marshal don't have any evidence even if he did live, Governor. Maybe this ain't as bad as it looks." Lock's meek intrusion only made Cornell more angry.

The governor seemed to deflate and he collapsed into his chair. "We're going to have to be very careful for a while. We need to get this trial over with and lay quiet until all of this blows over."

Jasper sat on the bunk in his cell. He knew things would come to a head tomorrow or the next day and he had to be ready. He stood and walked to the cell door.   No one was around.

He sat back down and lifted the fringed leather flap around the top of his left moccasin. He removed a .41 Remington double barrel derringer from the pocket and checked the loaded rounds. Satisfied they were in good shape, he put the gun back in his moccasin.

The right moccasin held his dirk. He ran the blade lightly over the top of his hand, shaving hair. It was razor sharp. He put it back into its sheath.

Jasper leaned back against the wall and thought of Gale. He wished he could hold her and tell her how much he loved her. He was playing a close game that he just might lose.

He didn't know just when he would make his move. He would only get one chance. Things needed to come together just right.

Bart Moore and the governor had to be within gun range and he needed a horse for his escape.

His thoughts turned to Willis. If he didn't show tomorrow he was likely dead. Jasper hoped not. He was getting to like the little guy.

The sun was setting when Stan and his group met Claw Of The Eagle leading a group of riders and wagons about two miles from Kentville.

"Stan Barstow, this is my sister, Gale Lee," the warrior said. "Gale, Stan Barstow is the United States Marshal."

Stan tipped his hat. "Nice to meet you, Mrs. Lee."

She held out her hand and gave him a firmer handshake than he expected. "Nice to meet you, too, Marshal. We're here to get Jasper and take him home." Gale Lee sat with her back straight as an arrow, her jaw set firm under flashing, defiant eyes.

"I'm sure you are, Mrs. Lee."

Stan turned to the group that spread across the road and took up a quarter of the field. "Folks, we're dealing with very dangerous people. How many here are armed?" Everyone, including the women, raised their hand. "All right, I have federal warrants for the arrest of Governor Cornell Norris and his gang, but we have to approach the situation carefully."

He turned to Captain Anthony. "Captain, could you and your men take these folks to an encampment until morning? We don't want to arouse suspicion with this group getting there all together."

"We'll take care of it, Marshal."

"Folks, I want you to follow the soldiers to a place where you can camp for the night. I expect they're going to try to hang Jasper tomorrow or the next day. When they move him to the gallows we'll move in and arrest them all as they should all be there. Black Feather, Wind Runner and Claw Of The Eagle are my deputies...follow their directions."

Claw Of The Eagle looked from Stan to Black Feather to Wind Runner and back again.

Wind Runner showed him the badge on his chest.

"I need to swear you in as a deputy US Marshal." Stan handed the warrior his commission papers. "Raise your right hand."

The clan members with the party murmured excitedly.

Claw Of The Eagle nudged his mount to Stan who swore him in as the clan members looked on with beaming faces.

"Marshal," Gale Lee said after the swearing in was complete, "you should know that my husband is the Sheriff of Cassidy County."

"What?"

Al Dolan sat up in the bed of the wagon Gale was driving. "Marshal, my name is Al Dolan. Claire Dolan, my daughter, was raped and murdered by Bart Moore and his men. We appointed Jasper sheriff so he could go after them as a lawman."

"How come he didn't tell me that in Lowell Town?"

"He doesn't know it yet."

Stan laughed. "There sure is a lot of appointing going on without the appointee knowing about it. Well, this is going to make things even more interesting."

"Marshal, the man in the litter is Harry Wells. He used to ride with Bart Moore, he has evidence," Claw Of The Eagle said.

Stan dismounted and walked over to Harry. "You know something about Moore, Mr. Wells?"

"I do. I heard him braggin' about killin' Jasper's kin and the Dolan girl. I don't want to say everything he told me in front of the girl's kin. He also allowed how his uncle, the governor, was goin' to solve his problems, includin' gettin' rid of Jasper."

"Will you testify to that?"

"Yes, sir, Marshal. I surely will."

Stan got back on his horse. "Okay folks let's get moving."

It was after nightfall when Stan and his deputies brought Willis to Doctor Scoville's house. Stan knocked on the door and after some time, Doctor Scoville answered.

"What is it?" He held a lantern high enough to shine in Stan's eyes.

"US Marshal, Doctor. Sorry to disturb you, but I have Willis Harwick in that litter. He's been shot in the head."

"Lord, I warned him not to go." The doctor hurried to the litter. He held the lantern over Willis' head and moved the bandages. "We need to get him inside."

Stan and Wind Runner carried Willis into the house.

"This way please." Dr. Scoville led them to the back of the house to his clinic room. They lifted Willis from the litter and laid him on the examination table. In the light of the room Stan could see the doctor was taken aback by Wind Runner's size and fierce visage.

"Doctor, my name is Stan Barstow and this man is one of my deputies, Wind Runner."

The doctor nodded and turned to Stan. "Marshal, the rumor is you're dead."

"Almost, Doctor, but thanks to my new deputies I survived the attack."

Scoville waved smelling salts under Willis' nose and the young lawyer jerked to consciousness.

"Willis, it's me, Amos."

Willis looked around until his eyes focused on the doctor. "Amos, it's good to see you."

"It's good to see you, too, Willis, as I thought I might never see you again."

Willis squeezed his eyes shut. "Oooh, my head!"

The doctor went to a cabinet and took out a bottle of pills. He cut one in half and crushed one of the halves into a powder. He gave the other half to Willis with a glass of water poured from a pitcher next to the examination table.

"Here, Willis, swallow this. It will make your headache fade in a few minutes."

"What is it?"

"Opium."

The doctor poured water into the tiniest saucer Stan had ever seen then brought it and the opium powder back to the table. He dipped the end of his index finger in the water, pressed it into the powder, and gently rubbed the opium onto Willis' wound. Either the pressure of the doctor's finger or the sting of the opium caused Willis to take a sharp breath.

"Sorry," the doctor said, "but the pain will stop shortly."

The doctor finished applying the opium. "How's that?"

Willis made a crooked smile. "Feels better."

"Good. Now I can clean and treat the wound. It may still hurt some."

Willis took a deep breath. "Go ahead."

When Doctor Scoville finished, Stan approached him.

"Doctor, I imagine you have a feel for the townsfolk here."

"Yes, Marshal, I think I do."

"What do they think about the governor and his friends?"

"They're all basically despised. Unfortunately, the governor seems to be able to get the votes...or at least get the ballot boxes stuffed."

"I think I can solve that problem but I need some help. Do you have folks here you can trust?"

"Absolutely. Most people in this town are decent and law abiding. They want things to change but objecting in public can result in a short life span."

"The kind of help I need right now is not the public kind. I need people who can move around and in the courthouse so they can watch what's going on and report what they see to me."

"I know several good men who would be willing to do that."

"And I know several good women who would help also." Mrs. Scoville approached. "I'm one of them."

"Doris! What are you saying? I can't allow you to endanger yourself!"

Doris straightened her back and raised her chin defiantly. "Amos, this is a fight for what's right and that makes it everyone's fight."

"Ma'am, I must tell you as I will tell everyone, eventually you may have to testify in court."

"I'm well aware of that, Marshal. I'll be a very good witness."

Stan smiled. "I'm sure you will."

Dr. Scoville put his arm around his wife's shoulders. "Marshal, tell *us* what you need done."

Stan and Amos stood together in the darkness watching the last of the town volunteers disappear into the night. The moon was a sliver and a thick carpet of stars in the clear sky blanketed the earth in soft starlight. Stan hoped it was a good omen.

"Well, Marshal, how do you feel about our volunteers?"

"Good people, Doctor.

"Call me Amos. I think we've come to trust one another enough to be on a first name basis."

"Thank you, Amos. That's fine with me. I'm Stan. I think we'll have enough evidence to put these scum in prison for a very long time and hopefully even hang a few."

"I hope so, it's long overdue." Amos looked around. "Where's your deputy?"

"Working."

"I never heard of Indians being US Marshals before."

"Well they're mine and they all consider themselves brothers of Jasper Lee."

"Jasper Lee?! Now there's a complicated man for you."

"So I'm beginning to figure out. Quite frankly, I don't think I could've found three better men. They're fearless, smart and know their field craft. I'm damn lucky they came along when they did."

"Well, I know I wouldn't want Wind Runner looking for me!"

"And that, Amos, is exactly what I want everyone to think."

Amos nodded his head. "Stan, I think this territory is very lucky to have you as our United States Marshal."

"Thank you. I'll always try to live up to your confidence. I also need to talk to you about the Norton family you told President Grant about."

"There's not much to tell. They disappeared and Norris claims he bought their ranch and they went back East. I know that's poppycock. The Norton's would never have sold their place."

"They didn't. They were shot."

Amos' eyes grew wide. "How do you know?"

"One of Norris' men is turning prosecution witness. He was there."

Amos leaned hard against the porch rail. "God as my witness, Stan, I'll do whatever it takes to bring those despicable men to justice!"

Wind Runner eased next to Black Feather as he stood in the shadows of the building across from the saloon.

Black Feather pointed to it. "They are in there. Their sign showed they reported to the sheriff first. I think they are deputies."

Wind Runner's jaw tightened. "Stan has a good plan working. Many people here are helping. He wants us to find Bart Moore and Governor Norris and make sure they do not leave when he makes his move."

Chapter Twenty-One

STAN STOOD ON the Scoville's back porch sipping coffee and watched the orange tinged sun begin to appear from behind the mountain.

The door opened and Doris came out onto the porch. "You didn't get much sleep last night, Stan."

"Good morning, Doris. I got enough."

"If you're like me you can't sleep in a strange bed anyway."

"Yep," Stan agreed even though he slept in his bedroll which he was quite use to. "Your good coffee helps, though."

"Why thank you. I order it special from San Francisco. Amos likes good coffee. It's a good thing he's a doctor because he wouldn't like cowboy coffee."

"How do you know about cowboy coffee?"

"I was raised on a ranch. Started riding horses when I was five. Started working with the cowhands when I was eight."

"That's mighty rough work for a girl."

"It wasn't for me and the cowboys took good care of me anyway."

"Well, Doris, you're quite a lady. How'd you meet Amos?"

"We met at Willamette University. I was attending school and he taught one of my classes. We fell in love and he decided he wanted to practice in a rural area. Our plans were interrupted by the war, but we eventually made it here."

"Well, I'm very glad you decided to settle here. You both are wonderful folks."

Black Feather and Captain Anthony came out onto the porch.

"We're ready to get our people in position," the captain advised.

"Good. Filter them in a little at a time. Get some of the women into the courtroom...except for Mrs. Lee. She might not be able to contain herself. You might bring her here, Black Feather."

"I will."

"We'll get some advance notice that they will be heading for the gallows from other folks helping us out. As soon as they come out of the courtroom, start moving in."

"We'll be ready."

"Good luck."

"Stand up, Lee!" The sheriff jingled his keys as a taunt before he unlocked Jasper's cell. "Time to go to court."

They marched him out to a waiting wagon and stood him at the end of it. "Sit down." The deputy gave Jasper a push before he even had a chance to follow the order. Two men armed with shotguns walked in front of the wagon, two walked in the back with Jasper and two riders followed them on the hundred yard trip down the street to the courthouse.

A large crowd milled around the front and they parted as the wagon rolled to a stop before the door. An unsettling quiet hung in the cool of the morning. The same deputies shoved Jasper off the wagon hard enough so that he stumbled before he caught his balance.

On the walk down the aisle Jasper looked around the packed courtroom. A lot of people he didn't know, but he smiled and nodded at each person he recognized. Each returned the silent greeting, a quiet acknowledgement of their support.

The sheriff pulled out the chair at the defendant's table. The combination of Willis' absence and the smug look on the prosecutor's face turned Jasper's gut. Surely, Willis was dead. Jasper took a long breath in a futile attempt to lessen the weight in his heart. Blood pounded in his head. A good man had died in his defense. Someone else who needed him to apply natural justice. He looked around the room searching for the thing he wanted to see. He found it in the first row behind the prosecutor's table.

Bart Moore sat next to Governor Norris, both well within gun range. The sheriff removed the manacles and Jasper sat down. His hand moved toward the top of his moccasin. He knew he could kill them both, but he also knew he wouldn't live ten seconds after he did. The faces of Gale and his children floated prominent in his mind. His hand moved back to the table. He needed the third element before he took action...his means of escape.

The sound of the gavel shot from the bench.

"This court is now in session! The case of Territory versus Jasper Lee, Criminal Docket Number 17, is reconvened," the judge announced. He looked over at Jasper with a mildly triumphant look. "Mr. Lee, where is your lawyer, Mr. Harwick?"

"I suspect you know better than me, judge."

Muffled laughter rippled through the gallery.

The judge's face flushed crimson. "Watch your mouth, Mr. Lee, or I'll hold you in contempt!"

Jasper shrugged.

"Mr. Prosecutor, you may give your opening statement."

The tall, lanky prosecutor stood and Jasper noticed how different he looked from Willis. Jasper had seen it too many times before. A two dollar haircut and a twenty-five dollar suit finished off by a lesson or two in just the way to stand to look important. This man had no doubt been groomed by the governor for just such a purpose. Groomed to makes lies sound like the truth.

The prosecutor cleared his throat. "Thank you, your Honor. Gentlemen of the jury, this will be a simple case of cold-blooded murder by ambush. The Territory will present eye-witness testimony from Mr. Bart Moore, an upstanding citizen..."

"Bullshit!" A voice yelled from the gallery, which erupted in more shouts.

Bart Moore's face was purple and his mouth pulled in a tight line.

"Order! Order!" The judge slammed the gavel so hard on the bench, Jasper thought the wooden hammer might shatter. "I'll have order in this courtroom or I'll have the sheriff clear all of you out!" The judge glowered around the room.

"You may continue, Mr. Prosecutor."

The prosecutor wiped a shaky handkerchief across his forehead then cleared his throat again. "Gentlemen of the jury," he continued with a voice that matched his shaking hands. "The evidence will show Jasper Lee is a murderer..."

Silence reigned in the courtroom. The judge stared at the prosecutor like he was expecting something more.

The prosecutor fumbled with his papers, suddenly said, "Thank you," and quickly sat down.

The judge's eyes slid toward the spot where the governor sat.

Jasper noticed the governor made that little nod again when the judge leaned back in his chair and turned to the defendant's table.

"You may give an opening statement, Mr. Lee."

Jasper rose and instead of looking at the jury, he turned and faced the people in the gallery. "I'm not guilty of murder. There are times when natural justice demands swift and final action and without natural justice none of us is safe. This trial is about the choice of natural justice or the man-made perversion of it." Many people, even ones he didn't know, nodded their heads. He took his seat, satisfied he wasn't alone in the room.

"Mr. Prosecutor, you may call your first witness."

"Your honor, the Territory calls Mr. Bart Moore."

Moore walked up to the witness stand. He wore a neatly pressed black suit coat and a clean white shirt with a conservative black tie.

"Mr. Moore, please raise your right hand," the judge said.

Moore looked right at Jasper and one side of his mouth curved up. He raised his hand.

Jasper wanted to grab that tie around Moore's neck and squeeze until that smirk faded to nothing.

"Do you swear to tell the truth, the whole truth and nothing but the truth, so help you God?"

"I do."

"You may take the stand."

The prosecutor stood and walked to the witness chair. He seemed to have gotten control of his shaky hands. "Mr. Moore, can you please tell the jury where you were on May 17, 1873?"

"Yes, sir, I was camping on the trail with my friends."

"And where was your camp located?"

"Just this side of the county line, along Arlington Creek."

"Were you in Kent County?"

"Why yes, sir."

"And what, if anything, occurred while you were there?"

"We was ambushed."

"What happened?"

"Well, Jasper Lee there started shootin' and killed a bunch of my friends."

"Are you referring to the man sitting at the defense table?"

"I sure am!"

"Your Honor, may the record reflect the witness identified the defendant?"

"So ordered."

"Mr. Moore, what did you do when the shooting started?"

"What any smart man would do. I high tailed outta there."

"Thank you, Mr. Moore." The prosecutor turned to Jasper. "Your witness, Mr. Lee."

Jasper hesitated. He had no idea what to do except ask questions. He knew Moore was lying about the location and he knew Moore never saw him. The only truthful thing Moore said was that he ran as soon as the shooting started. Jasper decided to start from there.

"Mr. Moore, where did you go when you ran?"

"I came here, to Kentville."

"Did you report the ambush to the sheriff?"

"Hell yeah!"

"Right away, I take it."

"Yep."

"How did you know it was me?"

"I saw you."

"Where was I?"

"You was up on the mountain."

"What mountain?"

Moore shifted in his seat and ran the back of his hand across his mouth. "I don't know the name of it."

"Ain't that because there ain't no mountains this side of the county line?"

A murmur swept through the gallery and at the same time the prosecutor rose to his feet. "Objection! The defendant is badgering the witness, your Honor."

"Sustained."

"What does that mean?"

"It means I agree with the prosecutor."

"Since when is gettin' at the truth badgering the witness?"

"When I say so, Mr. Lee!"

"He's being railroaded!" A voice cried out from the gallery.

"Yeah!" A swell of angry voices began to rise.

"Order! Order! Sheriff, clear the courtroom."

"Everybody out!" the sheriff yelled as he and his deputies herded people toward the door. The gallery was emptied, but it didn't stop the flow of heated comments.

Jasper turned to the jury. Some of the men were looking down at the floor. Others were fidgeting in their seats with ashen faces. A few were wiping sweat off their brows.

Apparently Governor Norris recognized the same effect. "All right, let's get this over with!"

"Governor…" The judge tried to gain some respectability, but it was clear as day who was running this show.

"Shut up and get Morey on the stand!" Norris gave the court reporter a menacing look. "You better know what goes in the record and what doesn't."

The reporter nodded.

"Call your next witness, Mr. Prosecutor," the judge said.

"The Territory calls Sheriff Morey Lock."

Lock walked forward and took the oath.

"Take the stand," the judge ordered.

"Sheriff," the prosecutor began, "when did you become aware of the report of several men being murdered in the area?"

"When Bart Moore reported the crime."

"What day was that?"

"I don't know the date but it was a couple of days after the murders."

"What did you do?"

"I took a couple of deputies and went to where the murders occurred."

"Where was that?"

"Where Bart said it was."

"What'd you see?"

"A bunch of dead bodies, all shot."

"What was the evidence that led you to believe Jasper Lee committed the murders?"

"What evidence do you need? Jasper Lee is the only one who could'a done it."

The prosecutor stood silent for a minute, then he turned to Jasper and said, "Your witness, Mr. Lee."

"Thanks. Sheriff, can I see the notes you took at the place where these murders took place?"

"I don't need no damn notes. I know what I saw."

"Where was each man shot?"

Lock looked at the governor and then at the prosecutor. "My deputies did that work," he said through gritted teeth.

"Are the deputies who went with you in court today?"

"Uh, well, I don't..." A panicked look formed on the sheriff's face. "Ah, they're both dead...I mean Twittle's dead. Johnson is missing." Beads of sweat formed on the sheriff's forehead.

"Johnson is missing! Why aren't you and your men looking for him?" Lock's stare was hard and threatening.

"Actually, you're lying aren't you, Sheriff?"

"That's enough, Lee!" the judge bellowed. "Sit down. Mr. Prosecutor, start your closing argument."

Bart Moore left the courtroom by a side door. The jury was disinterested in the prosecutor's comments. The outcome of this trial was not in question.

Jasper considered his escape plan. He figured he would take action when the deputies took him to the gallows. The whole county would turn out as they always did for a hanging. His best hope now would be that when he made his move he would have allies in the crowd.

"Mr. Lee! Wake up and make you're argument!"

Jasper rose to his feet. He looked at the governor. He looked at the judge. He looked at the jury. "I'm not guilty of murdering anyone."

Chapter Twenty-Two

STAN LISTENED TO THE CITIZENS of the secret brigade report what they saw and heard.

Black Feather came in. "The governor's men and sheriff's deputies are spread all through the town, ready for trouble."

"Good. They'll get it, just not the kind they may be expecting. Make sure everyone is in place."

Black Feather nodded and went out the door.

Stan looked around for Amos Scoville, but he found Doris in the kitchen.

"Amos just went in to work on our patient." Doris pulled a loaf of delicious smelling bread from the oven. "Willis will need a little fixing up if he's going to have enough strength to make it into town."

"I was hoping Amos could go into town to find out what's going on with the proceedings."

"I know just the thing, Stan. Can you hook up the surrey for me? It's in the back so you'll not be seen."

Stan had a flash of uncertainty about sending a woman into such a dangerous situation alone, but he needed to know what was going on. "Certainly."

Doris came out wearing her bonnet and carrying her purse. "I just need to pick up something for dinner tonight."

She winked and climbed into the surrey. "Tell Amos I'll be right back."

Maggie Colson and her daughter, Emma, walked briskly back from the courthouse carrying the remains of the lunch they had served the jurors. They entered her café and found Doris Scoville waiting.

"Maggie, did you see any of what's going on in there?"

"Oh Doris, they are such horrible men. The governor is in there with them and they are just jokin' around. They don't care about any evidence and such. They're just goin' to hang Mr. Lee."

"I wonder why they're doing it this way instead of just lynching Jasper."

"I heard the governor say they had to make it look good, but Lord knows they ain't foolin' no one."

"Someone said they was goin' to hang Mr. Lee this afternoon," Emma reported. "I thought it was good to hang him, Mrs. Scoville. He's a bad man, ain't he?"

"I know he is a gunfighter, Emma, but so far I've only seen him do good things."

Emma's eyes started to brim with tears. "Oh. I feel bad he's gonna hang now."

Doris patted Emma's arm. "Don't fret, dear. No one is going to hang today."

Doris picked up her package and went home to tell Stan what she heard.

"Good work, Doris," Stan said. "It's time for me to show my face."

The judge banged his gavel. "The defendant will stand."

Jasper rose. During the time everyone was busy with the so-called deliberating, Jasper had moved his dirk from his moccasin to his sleeve.

The judge turned to the jury. "Has the jury reached a verdict?"

The foreman stood. "We have, your Honor."

"What say ye?"

"Guilty on all counts."

"Thank you for your service. You're all discharged."

The men of the jury filed out of the courtroom.

"Well, Mr. Lee, do you have anything to say before I pass sentence?"

"You might as well just go ahead and finish this farce."

The judge's face reddened. "I hereby sentence you to hang by the neck until dead."

"When?" Jasper asked.

"Now," the governor said. "Before we get too big of a crowd."

"I sentence you to hang now, Mr. Lee." The judge banged his gavel one last time. "Sheriff, carry out your duty."

The sheriff fastened on the manacles and shoved Jasper down the aisle and out the door. Jasper squinted until his eyes adjusted to the bright afternoon sunlight. A warm breeze floated by him and a calmness trickled through his body. The shrill cry of a hawk pierced the air, drawing Jasper's eyes skyward.

"Hawk, I need your guidance," Jasper said to his spirit guide.

All that I've said is true. You will own this day. Use it wisely.

"Whaddya doin', Lee? Goin' nuts because you're goin' to...Shit! Where'd all these people come from?"

"Move it, Morey." The governor's voice drew Jasper back to the matter at hand. "Let's get this over with."

Lock pushed Jasper up the stairs to the noose. Jasper shook the dirk from his sleeve and laid the blade against the rope on his wrists.

"Hold it, Norris!" Stan Barstow climbed up onto the gallows followed by Black Feather and an Army captain. "United States Marshals. Move in men! Take them all into custody!" Stan grabbed the governor. "Cornell Norris, I have a federal warrant for you. You're under arrest."

"Unhand me," Norris bellowed as the marshal put him in manacles. "I'm the governor of this territory!"

"Actually, Norris, we all think you're just a pile of shit!" a voice yelled from the crowd.

"We have a federal warrant for you too, Sheriff Lock," Black Feather informed him.

The crowd openly laughed and cheered.

With the assistance of Amos Scoville, Willis walked up to Judge Iverson.

Even though the young lawyer looked pretty beat up, Jasper couldn't have been happier and he silently thanked the spirits and the Lord that Willis was still alive.

Willis held out a paper to the judge. "This is a federal warrant for your arrest." Wind Runner put manacles on the judge.

Iverson's face turned whiter than a bed sheet. "Oh my God, you're alive."

Lock tried to twist away from Black Feather. "You can't stop this hangin'! Lee's been found guilty and sentenced to hang. Everybody knows he killed those men when he had no right to!"

Jasper cut the rope binding his hands, bent down and pulled his derringer. With barely a breath he swung around toward Norris.

"Jasper! Don't!" Gale ran up the stairs followed by Micah Niles and Bill Newlin.

"Gale?" Her name caught on the happiness Jasper felt at the sound of her voice. "What are you doin' here?"

She smiled and touched his arm. "We've come to take you home."

"For your information, Sheriff Lock," Bill Newlin said, "Jasper Lee is the Sheriff of Cassidy County and had every right and duty to bring those men to justice."

"Put the gun away, Jasper," Gale said. "It's all right. Marshal Barstow has everything under control."

Jasper looked around before he put the gun in his pocket.

Gale took his hands and held them in hers. She pressed the sheriff's badge against his fingers. "The people of Cassidy County appointed you to be their sheriff."

"Gale, I ca…"

She put her fingers on his lips. Her deep emerald eyes held Jasper still and quiet.

"Yes, you can. The words in your letter told me you know that true justice is a hard thing to understand. You've talked about justice ever since I've known you. Sometimes I think it haunts you. Now you've seen how justice can be perverted by men in power. Take *this* badge and do it right. Do it right for the people who believe in you and trust in you. Do it right for our friends and neighbors. Do it right for our family. Do it right for me."

"I couldn't have said it better, Jasper." Micah looked at Jasper. "We need you. I wish there were more men like you."

Bill Newlin nodded his head.

Jasper took a deep breath and looked at the badge for a few seconds. Rain Water's words came to his mind. *Find the star and keep it close to your heart.*

He folded his fingers around the cool metal and nodded. He started to put the badge on his shirt, but Gale stopped him.

She took the badge and pinned it on him. Then taking the cuff of her sleeve, she burnished it to a shine. She stood on her toes and kissed him. "It's good to see you, Sheriff Lee."

Micah handed him his gun belt and Bowie knife.

Suddenly shots rang out down the street. Bart Moore ran out from the bank, a saddle bag slung over his shoulder. He leapt onto his horse and galloped off.

"That's the man who escaped the ambush on Marshal Barstow," Wind Runner shouted. He pushed his way through the crowd and sprinted to his horse. He mounted with a leap and was off after Moore. Black Feather galloped after them.

"Pa!" Sean led Coal to the gallows.

Jasper jumped on his big horse and started after his brothers. Sean was right behind, but Gale's voice pierced the turmoil.

"Sean! No!"

Jasper turned. "Stay here, son."

Sean looked at Jasper then looked at his mother then back to Jasper again. The disappointment was clear in his eyes, but he turned his horse and rode back to the gallows.

Chapter Twenty-Three

WIND RUNNER RODE CAUTIOUSLY but fast enough that he could see the dust up ahead. He didn't want to run his horse down.

Moore was riding hard. His horse wouldn't last long at this pace. Wind Runner followed until dust no longer rose in the distance. Moore's horse was probably played out, so Wind Runner slowed. The approach to his position had to be made carefully. With Moore reduced to traveling on foot he was as dangerous as a rattlesnake.

A horse whinnied in distress.

Wind Runner dismounted and unsheathed his rifle. Still hugging the boulders, he reached a point where he could see the exhausted animal. The horse was down covered in lather and panting shallow, rapid breaths. The horse twisted and kicked, too weak to stand. The animal was dying.

The warrior wanted to end the horse's suffering with a bullet but that would reveal his presence and position. The horse lay with its face towards Wind Runner, his eyes searching in panic. Then the eyes found him. The gelding tried to raise its head, but it flopped back down. The horse seemed to calm down, his eyes meeting Wind Runner's who couldn't stand to witness the animal's suffering anymore. He raised his rifle, placed his sights on the animal's forehead and fired.

Before the bullet found its mark Wind Runner had spun and retreated back along the boulders. Several rounds ricocheted from his last position, the bullets flying off with a whine and an angry buzz.

He reached his horse and walked it back to the cover of a cove of scrub oaks. Then he carefully left the cover of the boulders to scout a different route up the mountain where Bart Moore hid. Just as he spotted Moore's hiding place he heard horses approaching. He slipped back down the ridge into a crevice between the boulders. He heard two horses pass, then peeked out and recognized the back of his brothers.

"Black Feather. Fire Hawk." Wind Runner stepped out from his hiding place. "Good to see you, brothers."

"Wind Runner," Fire Hawk clasped his arm, "have you found Moore?"

"He is up on the mountain with a rifle. He rode his horse to death. I had to shoot it."

"Where'd you see him last?" Fire Hawk asked.

"About two hundred yards up the mountain from a gap around the end of the boulders."

"We need to approach him from different directions." Fire Hawk thought for a minute. "One side can safely advance if he's kept busy on the other side. You two start up from here. I'll wait for your shots then gallop past the gap and start up the other side. That will give you a chance to gain some ground on him."

Black Feather dismounted and tied his horse next to Wind Runner's. He pulled his rifle out of its scabbard, stepped over to Fire Hawk. "Be careful, brother."

Jasper nodded. "You, too."

Jasper waited. The sun was bright and a fickle breeze played with the leaves of the sycamores so green in the sunlight. He put extra rifle cartridges in his pockets. Five minutes had not yet passed when a shot echoed down the mountain. Jasper pulled his hat down hard and urged Coal forward. The big stallion reached full gallop just before the end of the boulders. Jasper lay low along Coal's neck urging him with a low voice into the horse's ear.

The crack of a bullet tightened Jasper's gut. Then another...and another smacked a large boulder and ricocheted when Jasper passed. Coal galloped across the gap.

Jasper sat up and reined in Coal. A deer trail wound up the side of the mountain. He jumped off, pulled his rifle and started up the mountain at a fast trot.

Catching a glimpse of Black Feather, Jasper signaled with the cry of an eagle. Black Feather stopped and looked then pointed his rifle. Jasper followed the direction of Black Feather's signal and saw Moore headed up a ravine. Jasper figured he could go another hundred yards before Moore would have a chance of spotting him.

The trail was steep and the muscles in Jasper's legs began to burn as he kept up his pace. Breathing came harder but he focused on his target and didn't falter. He reached the base of an outcropping and stopped. Gulping air, he took off his hat and wiped the sweat from his head and face. When he regained control of his breathing, he crawled out onto the outcropping.

The ravine was cut wide by a dry wash lined with yellow granite chunks and sun bleached boulders. The wash bed provided a rocky but passable trail shaded by scrub oak and knotty pine. Cliffs and granite walls the color of rust lined most of the ravine. He could see his Indian brothers climbing the other side of the ravine, slightly ahead. He looked for Moore but couldn't see him.

He pulled his telescope out from inside his shirt. He swept the glass in front of Black Feather and Wind Runner to make sure Moore wasn't waiting in ambush. Swinging the glass up the wash he caught some movement but lost it in the dense cover of oak and pine. A few seconds later he clearly saw Moore moving at a fast pace, but soon lost him again in the trees. The outlaw was at least a hundred and fifty yards in front of the lawmen and still moving fast. Moore had good cover and concealment. A clear shot would be difficult now.

Jasper looked further ahead and realized why Moore was headed that direction. At the end of the ravine a large granite wall dominated the area. A granite wall that provided high ground and the perfect defensible position. A twinge of fear wound through his gut. The way Moore headed up the wash made Jasper realize the outlaw had been here before.

Jasper continued up the mountain at a quicker pace now that he knew Moore's destination. He reached another outcropping and took another look in the ravine. Wind Runner was a couple hundred feet ahead of Black Feather and had reached the top corner of the granite wall on that side of the ravine. The warrior eased out and crouched at the edge of the cliff, scanning the ravine looking for Moore. He rose and turned. A shot echoed along the side of the mountain and Jasper saw a chunk fly off Wind Runner's left leg. He fell on his side and the momentum pulled him over the edge of the cliff. He managed to get a hold on to something Jasper couldn't see and hung there over the side of the cliff.

More shots rang out and Jasper spotted Moore behind a pile of granite. Jasper raised his rifle and fired two rounds, but he heard his bullets ricochet. He turned back to where he'd last seen Black Feather but couldn't find him. Jasper looked back to Moore's last position. He'd disappeared behind the granite. Jasper turned back to Wind Runner and sucked in a sharp breath.

Bright red blood poured down Wind Runner's leg. The young warrior struggled to pull himself up, his left hand slipped. He reached back up with his left hand, but it was too far. He grabbed his right arm with his left hand and tried to pull himself up that way, still he couldn't make it.

Jasper watched wishing he could reach out and grab the hand and pull his brother to safety. He prayed to the spirits to give his brother strength to win this battle. But Wind Runner's hand slowly, slipped off the cliff. His fall was silent until it ended with the thump of his body on the boulders sixty feet below.

Jasper held back his pain like Pa had taught him, but inside a torrent of tears roiled together with his anger. When he finally regained control he noticed that he didn't see Black Feather anywhere. He called out the eagle cry.

No answer. That meant Black Feather was probably down as well.

Rage and heartache pushed Jasper up the mountain. The colors of the mountain became intense hues of bright emerald trees, glowing gold granite, flaxen tinged sand and stark white boulders. But there was no beauty in it. His only interest now was justice for his fallen brothers.

Jasper reached the corner of the granite wall. He hunkered down behind some boulders and took a minute to collect himself. He had lost his objectivity. Lesson learned...but it had been a costly one. Slow deep breaths soon calmed his rage. The criminal turned out to be a much better fighter than Jasper had believed.

Jasper surveyed the layout. The boulders that gave him cover also blocked his view. He got up on his haunches and listened. His ears sorted through what little noise he heard...the breeze, rustling leaves, swaying trees. The birds were quiet and the animals were still...Moore was close. Then, a loose stone to the right.

Jasper moved around the left side of the boulders, perilously close to the edge of the cliff. He sidestepped around the end of the boulders when Moore burst into view from the other end and fired his rifle from the hip. A bullet smacked the boulder next to Jasper's head, spraying the right side of his face with rock and bullet fragments.

Jasper pitched forward to avoid going over the cliff and rolled to a kneeling position as Moore fired again and missed. Jasper's right Colt instantly came up in his hand spitting flame and lead. Moore staggered, dropped his rifle and ran behind the boulder.

Blood blinded Jasper's right eye and he pressed his body against the boulder, his heart pounding in his ears. He could hear Moore running away, then saw him cutting to the left through the live oak. He wiped his eye with his sleeve and started after his prey.

Jasper took his time. Moore's trail was easy to follow, but he was wounded and every hunter knows a wounded animal is the most dangerous animal. Maintaining the best cover and concealment he could, Jasper tracked the signs step after careful step. Every detail appeared in sharp focus and he caught every movement...heard every sound.

The trail led to a cave about a hundred yards from the edge of the cliff. Pain, anger and even fear wove through him as he tried to clear his blurred vision. He picked a position with good cover and waited, fighting a woozy feeling, fighting to keep the world from spinning into a deep black hole.

Bart Moore sat against the stone wall of the cave watching the outside. He tried to bandage his arm with strips torn from the bottom of his shirt, but the blood continued to seep through the cloth. Each breath came out in grunts and whimpers. After tying the bandage he threw the bloody sleeve he tore off to the back of the cave. He put his pistol in his left hand and stared out the cave entrance.

Pent up frustration and emotion erupted and surged through him. He screamed and began kicking the cave floor with the heels of his boots. Then he stopped, his chest heaving, tears running down his face... abandoned and alone again. *Mother, why did you bring me into this lousy world when you knew you couldn't love me? Why'd you give me up to father when you knew how evil he was, you bitch? Why?!*

Anger coursed through his veins. He wanted to kill everybody, but most of all he wanted to kill Jasper Lee. Bart pictured his bullet smashing into Lee's head as he stared out of the cave...waiting. After a few minutes he heard a sound in the back of the cave. He peered into the darkness. Nothing there. He turned back to look out of the cave. A low growl caused cold fear to coil up his spine. He turned to see glowing eyes rushing toward him. He fired, the flash blinding him. Ripping pain engulfed his arm from razor sharp teeth closing around his hand and tearing it off. He screamed...and screamed...and screamed.

The shot jolted Jasper. Then he heard Moore screaming and the growls of wolves. He listened trying to figure out what was going on, then it dawned on him. Moving cautiously to the side of the cave entrance he listened to the screams fade to gurgling whimpers, then nothing. Jasper moved just enough to peer inside the cave over the barrel of his rifle.

Moore was still alive, his mouth moving but saying nothing.

The wolves fed on the contents of his ripped open stomach. His white face, colored only with streaks of scarlet turned toward Jasper. Moore gasped and a hissing whisper came from his throat. "Shoot me."

The two men's eyes locked for a few long seconds. Then, without a word, Jasper turned and walked away.

Chapter Twenty-Four

JASPER SLOWLY WORKED his way down the other side of the ravine. He passed the corner of the granite cliff where Wind Runner fell, resisting the urge to look at his brother's broken body. He would see it soon enough.

When he got the place where he last saw Black Feather, he called out, fearful he would get no response. "Black Feather! Where are you?"

"I'm here, brother."

Relief flooded through Jasper as he raced toward the pain-laced voice.

Black Feather was propped up against a boulder in a short gully. His left foot was twisted at an odd angle. Jasper knelt and examined the splintered bone that had broken through the skin. "What happened?"

"I was running to Wind Runner when a boulder I jumped onto slipped. My leg jammed into a crevice. I could not stop my fall."

"You did well to stop the bleeding. I need to make a splint."

"Wind Runner?"

"Gone."

"Moore?"

Jasper looked at his brother. "Natural justice caught up with him."

Black Feather cocked is head.

"Wolves got him."

Black Feather grunted his approval.

Jasper cut some saplings with his Bowie knife and fashioned a splint with strips of the green wood. "How's that feel?"

Black Feather nodded.

"I'll make a litter."

"No, brother. I can make it down with your help."

"Your leg is in bad shape."

Black Feather eyed Jasper's head. "You are not doing so well, either. We will make it together."

The trek was slow and treacherous. When they reached the horses, they drank deep from canteens. Jasper wrapped Black Feather in a blanket and built a fire. He made sure no fever had risen then set food and water in reach.

"I'll be back as soon as I can."

"I'll be here," Black Feather replied.

Jasper led Coal up the ravine to the base of the cliff. He traveled up the wash and threaded his way through and over the granite chunks. The sun was being pulled to the western horizon when he reached Wind Runner's body.

Wind Runner lay face up. His eyes were open and even though the sun had begun its work, Jasper could see the peaceful set of Wind Runner's face.

No more battles, my brother. No more battles.

Jasper worked quickly to wrap the body in his bedroll blanket. He struggled to get the dead weight of the big warrior over Coal's back, but he was finally able to secure the body with rope and start down the mountain.

Halfway down the ghostly shadows of two riders approached.

"Jasper! It's Stan Barstow and Claw Of The Eagle," one of the rider's shouted.

"Hold fast. I'm comin' down."

When Jasper reached the men, Claw Of The Eagle dismounted and walked over to Coal. He patted the stallion's neck and ran his hand down along Coal's back until it reached Wind Runner. Claw Of The Eagle took a deep breath, laid his hand on the body and put his forehead on the blanket. Looking up he chanted in the words of the ancient ones. *Rise into the night sky, Wind Runner, and take your place at the campfire of all the great warriors, for you are truly one.*

He turned, put his hand on Jasper's shoulder, and held out the reins of his horse. "You ride, Fire Hawk."

"Thank you, brother, but I'll finish what I started. It's my way."

Claw Of The Eagle nodded and climbed back on his horse.

Stan leaned toward Jasper. "Black Feather says Moore's dead."

Jasper nodded. "Wolves. Don't worry, Marshal. There won't be much left to bury."

"I'd take it kindly if you'd write a report."

"I believe it's part of my job, now."

Stan smiled. "You know Sheriff Lee, I think you're going to be a damn fine lawman."

"I suppose. We best get movin'."

The campfire at the bottom of the mountain soon came into view. Jasper could see a wagon in the flickering blaze. A figure came from around the other side.

"Jasper?"

The sadness in Jasper's heart lightened. "I'm here, Gale."

In an instant her arms were around him, her head buried in his chest. He held her tight, like he would never let go. They stood quiet for a minute. Jasper savored her touch, her fragrance.

Then she looked up at him and brushed gentle fingers over the right side of his head. "Black Feather said you were hurt."

Jasper laughed softly. "My brother talks too much."

The rising sun was just beginning to golden up the sky when Stan, Claw Of The Eagle and the soldiers started the trek to Fort Hurley with the prisoners. The clan followed to make sure justice was done.

"We're all ready to go," Gale said to Jasper.

Their friends and neighbors from Cassidy County milled around waiting to make the return trip home.

Jasper shook his head. He couldn't believe the whole of Arlington had turned out. He knew now how much of a responsibility it was to be sheriff. These were the people who were counting on him to maintain law and order. He promised himself he'd give them his best. "You all go ahead," Jasper said. "I made a promise I have to keep."

Gale squeezed his hand. "We'll wait."

Doctor Scoville directed him to a little house at the north end of Kentville. Jasper dismounted and walked to the porch of the house Doctor Scoville had directed him to on the north end of town. He took off his hat and ran his hand around the brim. He couldn't remember too many things harder than what he was about to do.

His knock sounded hollow against the front door of the little house. After a few moments footsteps tapped across a wood floor. The door opened and a middle-aged woman peeked out.

Jasper took a deep breath, but it didn't break the tightness in his chest. "Mrs. Albright?"

"Yes."

"I'm Jasper Lee, Sheriff of Cassidy County. I'd like to come in and talk to you about Lawrence, if I might."

A man appeared behind her. He gently moved her aside and opened the door. "Come in, Sheriff."

Jasper stepped into a clean, orderly modest room. Mrs. Albright sat on a sofa, her hands gripped tightly in her lap like they could never be parted again.

"Have a seat, Sheriff." Mr. Albright waved to a chair then sat next to his wife and put his arm around her.

Jasper took another breath. "There's no easy way to say what I got to say. I know because I got the same kinda news awhile back. Your boy has passed on."

Mrs. Albright let out a low sob and put her face into her hands.

"Did you shoot him, Sheriff?" Mr. Albright asked.

"No, sir. I didn't. He and four other men committed crimes in Indian country and the Indians caught them."

"What did they do to them?"

"You don't want to know that, sir. I have more important words from Lawrence himself."

Mrs. Albright raised her head. "Oh please, Sheriff, tell us what he said."

"He told me you were good folks. Good parents. He asked me to say he was sorry for all the trouble he brought upon you. He told me to tell you thank you for trying so hard and that he loved you."

Mrs. Albright put her head against her husband's shoulder and sobbed softly.

Albright looked over at Jasper, tears streaming from his eyes. "We tried to raise him right, Sheriff. It's just he had somethin' in him that he couldn't control. He was always needin' to be contrary."

Mrs. Albright looked up. "Did he suffer, Sheriff?"

Jasper looked at her for moment trying to figure how to make the truth an acceptable answer. "Yes'm he did, but because he asked the Indians for forgiveness they spared him the worst of it."

"Then he died like a man?" Mr. Albright asked.

"Yes, sir. He did. He faced up to his deeds, accepted his punishment and died like a man."

Mr. Albright nodded. "Is there a grave?"

"No, sir…ashes to ashes."

Albright hugged his wife. "It looks like he had some decency in him after all, dear."

Jasper stood. "If you've no more questions, I'll leave you folks be."

Albright stood and shook Jasper's hand. "Thank you for coming and telling us these things, Sheriff. I know you didn't have to."

"I told him I'd come, sir. I always keep my word."

Jasper, Gale, Sean and Claw Of The Eagle rode into the clan village with Wind Runner's body. Everyone ran to greet them, but as the rest of the clan came forward Butterfly Wing stood back. Moon On The Water wrapped her arms around Claw Of The Eagle's leg. He leaned down and whispered in her ear and Moon On The Water looked over at her sister. Butterfly Wing turned and ran to her lodge. Moon On The Water went after her.

"Pa!" A chorus of voices greeted him. Rain Water followed behind the younger Lee children.

Relief and joy flooded Jasper's heart. He climbed down and gave each child a hug.

When the children moved on to hear what tales Sean had to tell, Rain Water came up and gave Jasper a hug.

"Mother."

"Where is my first son?"

"He broke his leg. The white man's doctor in Kentville is treating him."

Jasper's breath eased out through his teeth. "He had a bad break, Mother. The bone stuck out of his leg. He needs the hand of a good surgeon and Dr. Scoville is one of the best."

"Dr. Scoville?"

"Yes."

"I have heard of him from other healers. It is said he has the touch of a medicine man." Rain Water turned toward the wagon but she called over her shoulder. "I will forgive you this time."

Jasper smiled and followed her. "You forgive me every time, Mother."

Rain Water lifted the blanket covering Wind Runner. "Did he die like a warrior?"

"Yes, but we let our hatred for Moore cloud our judgment. Wind Runner took a chance and it cost him his life."

Rain Water shook her head. "Hate always hurts the one who hates," she said almost absentmindedly. "We must prepare his body."

The bottom of the deep orange sun was shaved off by the horizon when the clan sent Wind Runner to the spirits. Moon On The Water and Claw Of The Eagle each held one of Butterfly Wing's arms for support. When the ceremony was done the clan returned to their lodges. Jasper and Harry sat around the campfire.

"You're lookin' stronger," Jasper noted.

"I am stronger. As much as I'd like to stay I don't think I should use up too much of the clan's kindness. I might need it again."

"Where do you think you'll go?"

"I thought I'd stick to my original plan and leave the territory. I think I've been branded by ridin' with Moore. Work will be hard to come by around here."

Gale came out of Black Feather's lodge and sat between the men. "The children are asleep. Sean's pretty tuckered out."

"He did well in this crazy mess, watchin' everything while I was gone."

Gale looked into the fire. "Mother has named me."

Jasper smiled. "Who are you?"

"Swirling Wind."

Jasper laughed. "That's a fine name for you. Harry was tellin' me he's headin' out of the territory."

Gale squeezed Jasper's hand.

"Harry, Gale and I been talkin'. We now have two ranches to run and with me being sheriff, we're goin' to need help. If you're a mind to we'd appreciate it if you'd join up with us."

Harry sat quiet for a minute. Then he took off his hat and ran his sleeve across his eyes. "Damn smoke is gettin' in my eyes." He said nothing for a moment more then he looked at them with level eyes. "Folks, I'd be plumb proud to work for you."

"We were thinking about a partnership," Gale offered. "You run Pa's ranch and we'll split the profits sixty/forty."

"Well, ma'am, forty percent is mighty generous of you!"

"No, Harry, you'd be doin' most of the work. You'd get the sixty percent."

Harry's lips quivered and he made no attempt to hide the tears streaming down his face. He wiped them away and regained himself. "Ain't no one ever put stock in me before, not that I earned any. I'm forever indebted to you."

Gale touched his hand. "True partners are never indebted to each other, Harry."

The next morning, Jasper, Gale, the children and Harry were getting ready to leave. Jasper was on Coal and Gale, the younger children and Harry were in the wagon with Harry's horse tied to the buckboard. Sean was on his horse. They noticed the clan gathered around Butterfly Wing.

Rain Water walked over to Jasper.

"What's going on, Mother?"

"Butterfly Wing is leaving. No warrior will have her now. We told her she doesn't have to go, but she won't listen."

"Where's she goin'?"

"She does not know."

Harry climbed off the wagon. "Can I talk to her?"

Rain Water looked at Harry for a long uncomfortable moment, then nodded.

Harry walked up to Butterfly Wing and took off his hat. "Ma'am, Jasper 'n Gale have offered me a chance for a new life workin' their father's ranch. Well, I'm not too good at workin' by myself and I'd be appreciative if'n you'd come and help me out. I'll give you half my share."

She stared at him. "I am a ruined woman and brought bad spirits upon Wind Runner," she said as plainly as if she were discussing the weather.

"Sounds like we're two peas in a pod, ma'am, 'cause I ain't no prize bull my own self."

Butterfly Wing looked at the ground. "I could not do my woman duty with Wind Runner." She looked up at Harry. "I could not sleep with him."

Harry grinned. "Hell, ma'am, you wouldn't want to sleep with me anyway. I snore somthin' awful." His face turned soft as he held out his hand. "Come with me. We'll take it one day at a time and see what happens. If nothin' else, we'll just be in business together."

After a moment she took a tentative step toward Harry. He took her hand in his and they walked to the wagon together.

Rain Water looked at Jasper. "The Circle is unbroken."
He held out his hand and she took it in both of hers.
"You are no longer Fire Hawk. Your new name is Iron Star."
He nodded. "Thank you, Mother."
"May the spirits guide and protect you on your journey home."

Chapter Twenty-Five

IT WAS MID-SUMMER when Amos and Doris Scoville watched with warm hearts as Willis assisted Beth up into the buckboard seat. Willis was nearly fully recovered, but Beth still had a ways to go.

Willis had become Beth's therapist. His gentle soul and loving heart was leading her out of her darkness into the clean light of a new life. The hours he spent talking with her, walking with her in the woods and meadows in back of the Scoville's home, helped her get stronger. His calm determination to see her through her physical and emotional wounds was the best medicine she could ever have.

Beth settled in the seat and Willis patted her hand. He turned to Amos and Doris. "Well folks, I think we're ready to go."

Doris took Beth by the hand. "Don't overdo things, dear. Take your time. Now that your husband is a man of importance he can afford to hire help. Isn't that right, Judge Harwick?"

"Don't worry, I'll take good care of Beth."

Doris hugged Willis. "I know you will and she'll take good care of you."

Willis turned and took Amos' hand in a warm handshake. "Thank you for everything, Amos."

"No need to thank me. I was just doing what I'm supposed to do."

"Leading an insurrection isn't something you learned in medical school."

"Standing beside men like Stan Barstow and Jasper Lee...and you, made it easy."

Willis looked away for a moment. "Jasper Lee. My first and only client. I owe that man much."

"To me he just seems to be always looking," Amos said, "...always wary of something."

"He is a complicated man, but I don't think he's afraid of anything. I never detected fear during the time I represented him, just a natural curiosity and innate cunning that took in everything going on around him."

"Well, it's certainly a good thing to have him wearing a badge. He is well suited for the position."

"Unlike somebody else we know," Willis said, lowering his voice.

"What are you talking about, Willis? You'll make a fine judge."

"I'm not worried about being a judge...husband and rancher on the other hand..."

Amos put his arm around Willis' shoulders. "Both those jobs require a good heart, a good soul and a willingness to work hard. You have all the qualifications, Willis. You have nothing to fear."

Willis looked at Amos and smiled. "Thank you, Amos. You're a true friend."

They shook hands again and Willis climbed into the buckboard. Willis snapped the reins and the horse started down the road.

Doris took Amos' hand. "Is Willis nervous about Beth?"

"More nervous about himself. It's pretty obvious he's never been with a woman and given Beth's condition..."

"Amos, what is the most important thing in the world?"

He looked into his wife's eyes. "You know I believe the most important thing in the world is love."

Doris nodded. "Yes. Beth told me she loves Willis more than she loved Orrin. They will be fine and eventually what Willis needs to know, Beth will teach him."

"Well, then Willis is one lucky man!"

Doris stepped back and looked at her husband with a cocked head for a moment, then locked her arm onto his. "Well, Dr. Scoville, why don't we step inside and I'll teach you a thing or two."

Amos' face broke out in a boyish grin. "I do believe I'm one lucky man!"

It took ten months and three trials to finish all the cases against Cornell Norris and his co-conspirators. One trial was for federal corruption charges and two of the trials were before Judge Abramson acting as Kent County judge on charges of murder, attempted murder, grand larceny, kidnapping, and conspiracy for the crimes committed against Coy Jeffers, Rich Delton, Jasper Lee, and Willis Harwick. No murder charges were brought in the Norton case because according to Carlos' testimony, the men shot in self-defense. In the end, Norris, Rance Iverson and Morey Lock, along with the men who tried to kill Willis were sentenced to hang. All the others received long prison sentences, including the men on the jury in Jasper's fake trial. In exchange for life in prison, the prosecutor testified on behalf of the Territory.

Two months after the trials, Stan Barstow, Claw Of The Eagle and Jasper Lee approached the cells holding Norris, Iverson and Lock, the last of the criminals to face the gallows.

Iverson sat in the corner of his cell facing the wall, his head hung down on his chest.

"He's been sitting like that for days," the sergeant of the guard said.

"We'll have to carry him then," Stan said.

Two soldiers came in with a stretcher, loaded Iverson on it and took him out.

"C'mon let's get this bullshit over with!" Morey Lock growled.

Jasper clicked the same manacles on Lock's wrists that the ex-sheriff had used over a year ago on him.

Stan stepped up to Norris.

"Let's go."

Norris didn't move.

"This can go easy or it can go hard. Either way you're goin'."

"Alright, Marshal…I choose…hard!" He lunged at Stan.

Stan deflected a blow.

Claw Of The Eagle was there before Norris could throw a second punch. They lifted Norris off his feet and slammed him to the ground face down. Claw Of The Eagle held him down while Stan manacled his hands and feet.

"I won't go!" Norris yelled. "I won't go!"

"What an idiot," Lock said and stepped over Norris.

Soldiers picked Norris up by the hands and feet and carried him out.

Now and then the sun showed through gathering clouds. Three nooses swung in a strong breeze that carried the smell of coming rain. Iverson sat on the trap door, two soldiers waited behind him for the proceedings to begin. Lock stood tall as Jasper followed him up the gallows stairs. Norris sobbed and babbled something incoherent. Then he suddenly gathered his wits.

"I'm sorry I couldn't save Bart, Sis."

"Don't bother yourself, governor." A man in the crowd yelled. "He weren't worth savin' anyhow."

People in the gathered onlookers started to laugh and taunt. Norris' sister ran away.

Jasper offered Lock a hood.

Lock turned to him and shook his head. "It's a good day to die. I admire you for turning this whole thing around, Jasper. You're one tough son of a bitch."

"And I admire a man who has the sand to face his punishment."

"Appreciate that. By the way, I thought I'd do one good deed before I go to hell."

"What's that?"

"I heard Norris and his boys talking about the Norton shootin'. They were sayin' how Carlos didn't even pull his gun. Didn't fire a shot. I thought some lawman oughta know Carlos is tellin' the truth about that."

The two men nodded to each other.

Nooses were slipped over bare heads. Knots tightened against necks. Moments later the hangman pulled the lever and ended the worst bout of crime since the cattle wars.

Three men stopped their horses on the crest of a hill overlooking the territorial border to the north. Carlos McElroy sat in his saddle, his hands bound. Sweat dripped from his head even though the morning was cool. They had been riding for two hours and neither Marshal Barstow nor Sheriff Lee had said a word.

Carlos played with his reins. "Marshal, can we just get this over with?" His voice cracked, embarrassing him even more.

"Get what over with?" Marshal Barstow said.

"Well, I figure you brought me out here to shoot me, which I appreciate because I don't want to do the danglin' jig in front of a bunch of ol' ladies, but we might as well get on with it." Carlos tried to moisten his dry mouth but he couldn't get together enough spit to wet a postage stamp.

"I didn't bring you here to shoot you, Carlos."

"You didn't?"

"Nope."

Relief blew the tension out of Carlos' body so fast he started shaking and almost fell off his horse. Sheriff Lee reached over and steadied him in his saddle.

"W...w...why?"

"First off, you were true to your word and testified against all those men. I don't believe we could've convicted all of them without you. Secondly, you didn't whine or bug me for leniency. You took responsibility for your crimes and were willing to take whatever the judge was going to give you. But mainly, during our many conversations over this last year or so, you've told me you were sorry for what you did"

Carlos hung his head. "I am truly sorry for my crimes, especially the Nortons."

"Why?" Sheriff Lee said. "You didn't shoot them."

"I'm sorry for what I didn't do. I should have stopped it."

"You would've died there with them," the marshal said.

The men were quiet for a good while. The plains stretched out before them to a faint line of blue mountains in the long distance. They watched the wind play with the prairie grass that had turned its autumn gold.

"One good thing about the West," the marshal finally said, "is that a man can put enough miles between him and his past to start a new life with a different name... if he can keep from the outlaw side of things." The marshal reached over and untied Carlos' hands. Then he reached in his saddle bag and took out a gun belt and a sack. "Here's your gun and some provisions."

"And here's your rifle." Sheriff Lee held out Carlos' Winchester.

"I told the judge I believe if given a chance at a new life you'd do well," the marshal continued. "You're getting that chance. Don't prove me wrong."

Carlos put the rifle in the sheath on his saddle and strapped on his pistol belt. He held his hand out. "Thank you, Marshal. I never thought I'd get a second chance. I won't waste it." He turned to Sheriff Lee. "I'm glad to have met you, sir."

"Good luck."

Carlos started down the hill toward the prairie, then reined in and came back. "Would you boys take offense if I could get hired on as a lawman somewhere?"

Stan shook his head. "Take whatever job suits you."

Carlos touched the rim of his hat and headed for those distant mountains.

Stan and Jasper watched Carlos shrink in the distance.

"Do you think I did the right thing, Jasper?"

"I understand why you let him go, but I'm kinda mixed up inside about it."

"Well, he did over a year in jail on top of everything else. The judge was going to put him in prison for twenty years. He would've gone to the same prison as some of the people he testified against. Wouldn't have lasted a month. I just didn't think it was right. Besides, the only man he murdered was Rich Delton."

Jasper let out a long breath. "Thinking like that makes this star mighty heavy."

"It's supposed to be heavy." Stan touched the badge on his own chest. With a man like Jasper Lee on his side, it didn't feel quite as heavy as it used to. "That piece of metal on your chest doesn't make you better than anyone, it just means you've accepted the serious responsibility that comes with it."

"Yeah, I know. My deputy is philosophical about the job. He tells me the same things you do. "

"I knew there was a reason I liked Sandy James."

They headed back towards the Ft. Hurley trail.

"I gave my final report on the Tully Valley shootings to the judge," Stan said.

"What'd he say?"

"Because these men committed such violent crimes you had good reason to believe they would continue to do so. The judge said you were justified in shooting them to prevent them from escaping and killing again. I did have a question about one of them, though."

"The young kid."

"Yes, the body was decomposing, but he did appear to be young. He had a bullet in the gut and one in the head."

"Moore put the one in his gut. I put the one in his head. He was still alive when I found him and hurtin' bad. I told him the wound was goin' to kill him and he asked me to finish him off.

For a long while the only sound was the clop of hooves, the creak of saddle leather and the occasional song of a bird.

"That was a tough thing to do, Jasper."

"The last look in that kid's eyes still haunts me."

"Oh?"

"I don't believe he was a bad kid. Life just never gave him a chance...but I'd a shot him if Moore hadn't."

"Those eyes," Stan said after a while, "they'll probably always haunt you, my friend."

Chapter Twenty-Six

JASPER TOPPED THE HILL where the passed over members of the Lee family rested. A distant, dark grey thunder storm crawled over the land, the wind animating the trees and grass to a spring dance flashing emerald and jade. Shafts of gold and orange from the setting sun found their way through gaps in the clouds casting Gale's shadow long down the hill.

Jasper pulled up next to his wife and dismounted. Coal and the mare nuzzled each other, passing whispered secrets.

"Sean said I'd find you here."

Gale turned to him, tears streaming down her cheeks into a peaceful smile. "We live in such a beautiful place, Jasper."

He pulled her close enjoying the feel of her in his arms. "This view feels a lot better than a year ago."

"That was a hard day in many ways. Thank God that terrible time is over. I can't believe it was so long ago."

"All we have to do is look at our children."

"Oh Lord, don't remind me. Sean not only acts like a man, he looks like one. And Megan is becoming such a fine young woman. And we can't make clothes fast enough for Brenden and Abbey. "

Jasper laughed. It felt good to laugh again. "Seems to be that way. I think we should enjoy our children while we can. Before we know it they'll be full grown."

Gale laid her head on his shoulder. "We've made a good life for ourselves. We've made the ranches into a good business."

"That we have, with the help of our children."

"Yes. Megan and Abbey are a great help around the house and yard."

"And Sean has done well runnin' the ranches with Harry...and Brenden."

They both laughed.

"I'm very proud of Sean," Jasper said. "Instead of bullin' his way in as boss, he knows Harry can teach him things. They've become good friends."

"Oh, I almost forgot to tell you. I visited Harry and Butterfly Wing. It appears they've become *very* good friends. Butterfly Wing is expecting."

Jasper laughed. "Well, I guess Harry doesn't snore so bad after all."

Gale punched Jasper in the shoulder. "Stop it. They look very happy together."

"Well, we best get them to the clan so Walks With Bears can join them."

"I know. I need to visit Rain Water again, too. I see so many things in a different way since my vision quest."

"You want to talk to me about it?"

"Not just yet."

Gale put her head back on Jasper's shoulder. "I love you, Jasper."

He lifted her chin and kissed her deeply, but gently.

Gale's face broke into a bright smile. They embraced and held it for a time. Jasper enjoyed the warmth spreading from the fire in his loins that holding Gale always brought. *God, how I love this woman.*

"We best be gettin' back to the house," Jasper finally said. He helped her mount her horse and he climbed on to Coal. They took one last look at the sunset and turned, their long shadows stretching into the fading light toward home.

The End

MORE GREAT READS FROM WHIDBEY WRITERS GROUP PRESS

GOTU by **Mike McNeff** (Action) When a drug cartel attacks a cop, the rules apply. When they attack a cop's family? There are no rules. An action-packed thriller written by a 40-year law enforcement veteran.

Necessary Retribution by **Mike McNeff** (Action) After two years of training by the best special ops teams in the US military, Robin Marlette and his team of ex-cops enter the world of covert operations and international counter-terrorism in this thriller.

ANTHOLOGIES by Whidbey Writers Group

Beneath the Rain Shadow (1994)

Beneath the Rain Shadow II (1996)

Beneath the Rain Shadow III (1999)

Take Our Words for Whidbey (2002)

Whispers in the Mist (2004)

Whidbey Connections (2007)

Whidbey Writes Again (2010)

Write Around Whidbey (2015)

www.ingramcontent.com/pod-product-compliance
Lightning Source LLC
Chambersburg PA
CBHW071527170626
46811CB00007B/2970